FAMILY PORTRAIT

Kern, Nannette Monson, Family Portrait

FAMILY PORTRAIT

NANNETTE MONSON KERN

DEDICATION

To my children: may you always remember the good times.

Forward

Hebrews 11:40

God having provided some better things for them through their sufferings, for without sufferings they could not be made perfect.

1 John 1:7

But if we walk in the light, as he is in the light, we have fellowship one with another, and the blood of Jesus Christ his Son cleanseth us from all sin.

CHAPTER 1 - *Tuesday, December 14th*

It was eleven days before Christmas, but for Nadine Collins it was just another twenty-four hours, like yesterday, or last week, or three years ago. Oh, the staff at the care center did their best to jolly up the residents in anticipation of the happy occasion: a Christmas tree in the foyer, evergreen garlands around the bulletin boards, carols over the intercom, even a Santa cap on the receptionist. Nevertheless, this was one lonely old woman whose heart the holiday spirit could not penetrate.

There had been a time when she'd reveled in the joyful anticipation. Even in the early days of her marriage, when money was virtually non-existent, the spirit of the holiday permeated her very core. She literally wore a smile from December first through New Year's Day.

There had, however, been one Christmas, a particularly destitute one, when she and her husband Melvin had resorted to resurrecting and refurbishing the children's old toys, and placing them under the tree. That had been the saddest yuletide of Nadine's experience. She could tell the children weren't fooled; it was clearly evident from their individual responses. Abigail had picked up the scrubbed and newly wigged doll with little interest, and Jimmy had drug his feet as he approached the freshly painted tricycle, which was secondhand when he got it the year before. Lisa's doll buggy held little attraction for her, even with the new lining. Tracey was only a few months old at the time, and because her activity of choice was crackling the discarded wrapping paper, at least one of her children was content. Not that the older ones complained. Even at their tender ages they seemed to understand the asperity of the family's situation. And, though they believed in Santa, they evidently didn't believe him to be of limitless resources. Or, soul wrenching thought: possibly they simply assumed that they hadn't been good enough to warrant any better.

With a sinking heart, on that long ago morning, Nadine had cleared away the meager traces of the disappointing fiasco, and disappeared into her bedroom, where she shed tears of regret. Then, fortifying herself with the thought that, "Things will be better next year," she pasted a smile on her face and began whipping up pancakes for their traditional Christmas breakfast.

Though finances had been a problem since the afternoon of the Collins's "I do"s, that Christmas was the only time that she had felt truly disadvantaged. Since then, the holiday season had unfailingly found Nadine restored to her characteristic high spirits. That is, until all of her joyful feelings were buried, along with her recent memories, deep within the irreparable confusion of Alzheimer's.

Her decline hadn't, of course, taken place all of a sudden. It began with intermittent bouts of forgetfulness and confusion, which gradually escalated, until about three years ago, when she fell and fractured her skull. Though she recovered physically, the initial trauma with its resultant surgery, along with the medications administered, forced her mind beyond the pale.

Many years before, while she was still of sound intellect, Nadine had instructed her family, in no uncertain terms, that they were to place her in a rest home, if and when the time came, and to have no regrets about it. She knew from personal experience how difficult it is to deal with a demented parent, and desired to spare her offspring as much of the ugliness as possible.

There were only three of her children left now: a son and two daughters. Lisa had died in her late teens, when she hit an icy spot on the road and plowed into the back end of a one ton truck. Danny, the unexpected child of mid-life, was reported "missing in action" after six months in Iraq. His whereabouts had never been ascertained, and the official presumption was that he was deceased. Nadine had nevertheless maintained hope, until her own condition became hopeless.

In spite of her formerly expressed wishes, the move to the care center had been a difficult and frightening experience, and Nadine continued to take out her frustrations on the long-suffering staff, as well as her own kin. On occasion, she seemed to accept her surroundings as those of her own home, often commenting to unrecognized family members about the chore it had been to re-upholster the furniture they saw there. She was also concerned, from time to time, about preparing dinner for the multitude of "house guests" who were occupying "her" living room. But, for the most part, she exhibited untempered anger, and demanded to be released "from this hellish den of demons."

Jimmy, her oldest, lived out of state, so was relieved of regular obligatory visits to the facility, but Abigail and Tracey faithfully took turns checking on their mother. Each ordeal–for that is what their visits had become–gave rise to further reflection, on Abigail's part, about the futility of it all. Their mother didn't know them, and was often verbally abusive; she seemed to take pleasure in harsh language and derogatory name calling. So, what was the use? However, "She's still our mom," Tracey would often remind her sister.

"She quit being our mom three years ago," was Abigail's standard reply. "But," she would sigh, "you're right. It's our duty."

Nadine, had she been aware, would have been appalled to know that she had become no more than a duty; the last thing she wanted was to be a burden to her children. She was, however, oblivious to their distress, as well as insensitive to their ministrations. They were merely part of the string of unknown humanity who annoyed her each day with their pushing, patting, lifting, and scolding.

Then, on the fourteenth of December, things changed. The day had begun as usual, with a strange young woman grabbing the handles of her wheelchair and steering her into the dining room, where she was surrounded by hordes of nameless faces. Who were all of these people, and why were they in her house? As she was rolled into place at one of the tables, she noticed the man on her left smiling at her, to which she responded by sticking out her tongue. Wasn't he a little long in the tooth to be flirting? Except that he didn't have any teeth, long or otherwise. "Don't get any ideas, you old goat," she grumbled. "If I wanted a man, I'd get myself one who didn't drool!" But her admirer seemed unfazed by her rudeness, and continued to grin. Nadine picked up a dinner knife from the table and waved it menacingly. "Listen, Buster, I lived on a farm for a long time, and the most fun I ever had was turning those would-be bulls into lily-livered steers. So just cool your jets."

"Nadine," came a cautioning voice from behind her. "Put the knife down. You don't really want to hurt anybody."

4

Nadine scoffed. "Oh, yeah? Says who?" Nevertheless, she tossed the utensil back to its place beside her plate, then twisted her body away from the would-be masher, giving him a frigid shoulder. Scrambled eggs and toast were soon placed before her, and the mild altercation was put out of mind as she concentrated on her food. Five minutes later she'd forgotten that there had been any kind of set-to in the first place.

The next order of the day was her shower, a chore she'd just as soon overlook. Why couldn't they simply leave her alone? All this fussing about was annoying, to say the least. And who wanted some kid pulling her clothes off, anyway? Nadine continued daily to battle against the onslaught, each time becoming more difficult to manage, but each time forced to succumb to the scrubbing.

No sooner had she been returned to her room than she was whipped right around and wheeled into yet another area, where she was shifted onto a padded board, to lie flat on her back while a young man moved her legs up and down. She supposed they were preparing her for the ballet, and therefore didn't strenuously object; she'd always loved to dance. As soon as she was limbered up, it would be time to go on stage and begin her routine. "What does the house look like tonight?" she asked her laboring assistant matter-of-factly.

"Full up, as usual, Nadine," the young man assured her good-naturedly, being accustomed to her favorite fantasy. "You'll knock 'em dead." By the time he had finished with her, however, she was too exhausted to perform. Her impatient audience would just have to wait until she was rested.

After lunch she was finally allowed some peace and quiet, if she could manage to ignore the constant outbursts from other residents. She ought to complain to the management. During her career with the dance troupe she'd traveled the world over, but had never before stayed in such a noisy hotel. People should have more consideration. Didn't they know who she was?

So, on and on, throughout the remainder of the day, her fancy gathered together the pipe dreams of a lifetime and created a glamorous milieu for Nadine's languor. Whether or not she could see through the diaphanous fabric of her make-believe world was anyone's guess. Be that as it may, the dream was much more palatable than her reality. Better to imagine herself as a prima donna with a throng of adoring fans and unencumbered by responsibility for anyone but herself.

She could almost see the curtains parting as her dancing feet carried her onto the stage. The audience would be standing in thunderous ovation as the opening strains from the orchestra filled her ears. So deeply engrossed was she in her illusions, she hardly knew when they'd taken her to her room that evening and put her to bed.

Nadine quickly fell asleep–it wasn't much of a transition–but awoke, as was her habit, in the middle of the night; this time, however, she was greeted by a new face. Needless to say, as far as she could tell, they were *all* new, but this one actually was. "Hi, Nadine. My name's Lisa. I'll be taking care of you tonight. So, if you need anything, now's a good time to speak up." She stood at the side of the bed, waiting for any requests.

Nadine's eyes, usually dull and unaware, almost twinkled. "I have a daughter named Lisa," she said with perfect clarity of thought. "As a matter of fact, today's her birthday." Nadine strained to make out the fuzzy features of her new care-giver. "My eyes aren't what they used to be, but I think you resemble her. You're about her size and coloring; she was a sweet little thing. We called her 'Meese' because she was so soft and gentle, so easy to please." Nadine shrugged and chuckled. "Don't ask me what one has to do with the other, but it seemed to fit. She was always cheerful, always laughing." Nadine smiled ruefully. "But, of course, even though it's her birthday, she'll never be more than nineteen."

Lisa lifted her eyebrows expectantly, and Nadine continued, "She died in a car wreck soon after my last child was born."

The nurse studied her patient's wrinkly features. "I'm so sorry."

"So am I. Not a day goes by that I don't think about her, and miss her. She was my peacemaker; everybody loved Meese."

A veritable stranger, the nurse actually had tears in her eyes as she said with sincerity and compassion, "That must be really difficult for you."

Nadine turned her head slowly from side to side, searching for a way to express her feelings. "There is no way to describe it." She huffed in frustration. "Words are useless when it comes to conveying that kind of emotion. Even after all these years, every time I think of my darling little baby girl being taken from me in that monstrous way, I feel like screaming my agony to the heavens. I've never stopped wanting her back."

"Well," soothed the nurse, as a tear meandered down one cheek, "you'll be having a happy reunion with her one of these days."

Nadine nodded, brightening somewhat. "Shouldn't be long now."

Lisa pushed the control that raised the head of Nadine's bed, fluffed her pillows, and settled the old woman more comfortably against them. Then, as she was smoothing the bed covers, she noticed the piece of jewelry that encircled Nadine's wrist. "What a pretty bracelet," she observed.

Nadine lifted her arm and smiled. "Yes, my girls gave it to me for Christmas five years ago. They always knew the perfect gift. Every year they've each added a new charm, even though, for the last little while, they've had no way of knowing that I was aware of their presents." The old woman's eyes misted. "It's my favorite little bauble. I've never taken it off." She hesitated. "When I go, will you be sure to give it to my oldest daughter Abigail? Maybe she and her sister can purchase another bracelet and share the charms."

"Of course," Lisa assured her. She then pulled a chair to the side of Nadine's bed and settled herself. "Why don't you tell me more about your family?"

Nadine smiled happily. "My favorite subject." Taking a deep breath, she began, "I'll start with Meese, since it's her birthday. She was only fourteen months older than Tracey, but she was more like a little mother than a sister. When she was only two, she'd get Tracey up in the mornings and have her diaper changed before I even knew either of them was awake. And it was always done with a light heart, out of pure love.

"One day I was in the kitchen, washing dishes, and happened to glance out the window just as Tracey crawled out the front door. But, not to worry! There was Meese, hot on her tail, wrestling the little scamp back into the house." Nadine chuckled and wiped at a tear.

"I worried for all of Meese's life that something would happen to her, that she'd die. I don't think it was a premonition; it was just that she had such a sweet, tender spirit, she seemed too good for this world. Even though I often lost my patience with the other children, I could never get upset with her. That's why I worried; I figured it just wasn't possible for anyone that close to perfection to stay on the earth very long."

Nadine pursed her lips. "She and I did go through a rough patch, just before she died. She was crazy about a young man that she met when

8

she was only fourteen. She never dated anyone else, and I didn't approve of them becoming so exclusive while still so young. I used to hide out in my bedroom when he'd come over, to make sure they were well aware of my disfavor." Nadine heaved a sigh of self-recrimination. "Five years of our time together I wasted in useless opposition. And then she was gone, and I never got the chance to apologize."

Her face clouded. "It was always hard for me to say, 'I'm sorry,' not because I didn't feel it, but because I was ashamed to admit that I had made a mistake in the first place. To me, there was never an excuse for my messing up—ever, under any circumstances—especially in cases where I knew better. And I always thought I should know better." She shrugged. "I thought I should know everything."

"No room for human error?"

"I didn't want to be human; I wanted to be perfect. And, when I fell short, it was easier to pretend it never happened, rather than to admit my flaws. So, since I never asked for Meese's forgiveness, I can only hope that she's given it to me anyway."

"She has."

Nadine looked askance at the young woman. "And how would you know that?"

Lisa smiled. "I think there's no place in heaven for condemnation. Your daughter wouldn't blame you for your human emotions. I'm sure she understands that you were only exhibiting motherly concern, though possibly not in the most suitable way."

Nadine sighed. "Sometimes I wonder if I ever did *anything* in the most suitable way."

"You did the best you could."

"But, was it enough?"

Lisa smiled. "It's all that's ever required. All humans fall short of the mark. I once heard it explained that it's like having a bank account with insufficient funds to pay your bills. You've worked hard, and done all you could to meet your obligations, but it just isn't enough. So you form a partnership with Christ, and he infuses your account from his own resources, and all that he asks in return is that you continue to give your best effort, and put in what you can. He will make up the difference."

Nadine cocked her head to one side, her expression quizzical. "And how did you get so wise at such an early age?" she marveled.

Lisa giggled. "I'm much older than you think."

"You can't be more than twenty," noted Nadine.

"Oh, you'd be surprised," Lisa countered. "But, go on, tell me more about this perfect daughter."

Nadine chuckled. "Yes, I know, you think I'm just a proud mother talking." She folded her hands across her mid-section and studied the ceiling, gathering her thoughts. "My other girls were blondes, but Meese was my freckle-faced little redhead. Unlike the stereotype, though, her temperament was easy-going and agreeable; she was a blithe spirit. You may not believe this, but I don't recall her ever becoming upset, or being down in the dumps over anything."

"Maybe she just didn't let you know."

"That's possible. But, like I said, she came pretty close to perfection." Nadine paused, and her shoulders drooped slightly. "A very regrettable memory I have is of one evening when I was angry with the other children for something—I don't even know what it was all about now. Anyway, I was determined that they would suffer for their childish transgression, so I refused to speak to them for the rest of the night. For some unknown reason, I included Meese in my shunning, even though she had been totally innocent of any wrong doing.

"I put them all to bed in silence, then went upstairs and crawled between my own sheets. A few minutes later, Meese came into my room—I think she was about four or five at the time—and stood at the side of my bed. 'Mama?' she said, the tone of her sweet little voice begging me to respond. And again, 'Mama?' Once more I ignored her, even though it was breaking my heart to do so. Finally, she left and returned to her room, and I cried myself to sleep." A tear slowly trickled down Nadine's cheek. "Why would I have done something so despicable?"

"Yeah, it's too bad you're the only person in the world who's ever made a mistake."

"Okay, but remember, Meese was the one who suffered because of my juvenile behavior," Nadine protested.

"Whenever we do something—" Lisa searched for a gracious way to put it.

"Stupid?"

"Well . . . ill-advised, we hurt those who are close to us. But, that's where forgiveness comes in. We're told to forgive those who offend us, even seventy times seven."

"She was just a little kid; what did she know about forgiveness?"

"There's no minimum age requirement for learning. When we're little, we're taught little lessons; when we're big, we get the big stuff."

"Even so, I'd give anything if I could take it back, do it over, act my age." Nadine lamented.

"I'll bet you never did it again."

Nadine scowled as she reflected, then slowly shook her head. "No, I'm sure I didn't."

"So you learned from it."

"I suppose so, but too late."

"Oh, it's never too late," Lisa refuted. "The time always comes when things can be made right. And Meese learned from it, as well."

Nadine scoffed. "What did she learn? That her mother was an idiot?"

"You're dwelling too much on the negative. It's not only others we need to forgive; sometimes the hardest person to let off the hook is ourselves. Try to focus on the good things you've done. I know there are happy memories. Tell me about those."

Nadine chuckled reluctantly. "You're right, there were lots of good times. I remember, when Meese was about nine months old, her favorite place during meal times was under the kitchen table. Abby hadn't mastered the art of feeding herself yet, and lots of good stuff was spilled on the floor by incompetent little hands. Meese was right there, ready to retrieve it. With all of that scavenging she should have been a chubby little kid, but she was always teeny, and even when she was grown, never weighed much more than ninety-eight pounds.

"She was also my songbird; without ever taking lessons, she had a beautiful voice and a good ear. We'd only been able to afford minimal training for her on the piano, but, if there was ever a song she particularly liked, she would sit at the keyboard and practice for hours at a time, until she could play it. She also sang duets with one of the little neighbor girls when they were about eight or nine.

"Our family was all musical, and did some performing when the children were little. When my girls were in high school, we sang together—my three daughters and I. We even took the blue ribbon at the Jefferson County Fair one year."

"You must have been pretty good."

"We did all right, I think, but Jefferson County wasn't exactly a Mecca of cultural refinement. As I recall, there was a distinct lack of qualified competition.

"Then, when Meese was a sophomore, she performed with the drill team, and as a senior, had the lead in the musical, 'Annie, Get Your Gun.' I'd never noticed before how much like me she was, but up on that stage–?" Nadine shook her head in wonder. "It was like watching myself. Eerie." She smiled ruefully. "On closing night, during curtain calls, the boy who played the part of Frank Butler tried to steal a kiss, but Meese ducked her head and refused. Poor kid, I felt sorry for him; he must have been mortified, there in front of all those people. I kind of scolded Meese afterwards, and told her she should have given him a little kiss."

"On the other hand," protested Lisa, "maybe it took a lot of courage, on her part, not to let the situation coerce her into something she didn't want to do."

Nadine tilted her head. "You show a good deal of wisdom for a mere pup."

Lisa shrugged. "I just know how I'd feel in that position, especially if my boyfriend was in the audience."

"What makes you think her boyfriend was there?"

"It stands to reason. You said they'd been together since they were fourteen. He surely wouldn't miss closing night."

Nadine studied the young woman beside her. It was uncanny how much insight she had, and how comfortable Nadine felt in her presence, almost like they'd known each other forever. Nadine huffed softly to herself, and then continued, "That same year Meese competed in the 'Miss Rigby' pageant, and performed with the Swing Choir, a very elite musical group at her school. I remember how proud I was, sitting there watching her sing and dance." Nadine laughed. "Except that her pants were too tight. She'd made them herself, and miscalculated slightly on the fit. Like I said, she was a teeny little thing, but nowhere near as teeny as those pants!"

Lisa laughed appreciatively. "I remember . . . once when something like that happened to me. By the time the night was over, I was sure my feet were turning blue." They chuckled together.

"The amazing thing was that, even with all of her talent, she was never too full of herself. She was a truly humble person, in the way we're all supposed to be: charitable, kind, long-suffering, not puffed up nor easily provoked. As I said before, probably more than once, she really was close to perfect."

"I'm sure it pleases her to know that you think so," Lisa noted, then seeing the look on Nadine's face, asked, "What?"

The old woman's expression was bemused. "It's just nice to have someone refer to Meese in the present tense for a change. Most people act as if she's only a thing of the past."

Lisa stood and patted Nadine's hand. "Well, I just figure that some people live here in Utah, some in New York, some in England, and some in Heaven. Just because we don't see those who are far away doesn't mean they don't exist." She smiled. "So, do you think you can sleep now? The sun will soon be up."

"Will you be here tomorrow night?" Nadine asked anxiously.

Lisa smiled. "Of course. I'll be here every night from now on, for as long as you need me."

Nadine relaxed and closed her eyes. "Good!" she said. "We can talk some more." Then with a girlish giggle she added, "Just remember, you're the one who suggested the topic. It'll be your own fault if I bore you silly."

Just before seven A.M., as Lisa was getting ready to leave, Abigail entered her mother's room. At her first sight of the nurse she gasped in astonishment. For a brief moment it seemed that her dead sister stood before her. She slowly blinked, thinking her mind was playing tricks on her, but the vision remained. Lisa held out her hand in greeting. "You're Abby," she stated matter-of-factly.

Abigail's brows shot upward as she took the offered hand. "Have I seen you here before?" she asked. "I don't remember meeting you."

"Last night was my first night," Lisa replied.

"But how do you know my name?"

Lisa smiled. "Your mother has been telling me about your family."

"My mother?" Abigail scoffed. "My mother doesn't even know who I am."

Lisa tilted her head and gazed at Abigail, still holding on to her hand. "She may not recognize you right now, but, believe me, she knows who you are."

"She talks utter nonsense most of the time. How could you communicate with her?"

Lisa shrugged, finally relinquishing her grip. "She was feeling good last night. We had a nice visit." Lisa smiled broadly at Abigail, as if she were about to burst into giggles.

"Did Mom say something about me that was funny?" asked the disconcerted Abigail.

"Oh, no," Lisa replied, still with a grin on her face. "It's just nice to see you."

Abigail observed in bewildered silence as Lisa patted Nadine affectionately on the arm, then lifted up her bed rails. Finally finding her voice, she declared, "You know, you look an awful lot like my sister."

Lisa turned and nodded. "That's what your mom said. I must have one of those faces. Well, I hope to see you again before–" She paused. "Well, before I move on to another job."

"So you don't plan to stay here long?"

"I'll be here as long as I'm needed, but I suspect I'll be moving on soon."

Abigail waited while Lisa disappeared through the door, then approached the bed and studied her mother's peaceful countenance. Was it possible that she had moments of lucidity? None of the other nurses had mentioned it. Did her thoughts miraculously unscramble only in the middle of the night? "Mom?" she spoke quietly. She could never tell, for sure, if her mother was sleeping or merely playing 'possum. Nadine's eyes fluttered open, a scowl immediately creasing her forehead.

"What do *you* want?" she groused. Well, at any rate, it appeared that things had returned to normal in the clear light of day.

"Mom," Abigail soothed, "it's Abby."

Nadine's eyes narrowed. "What are you trying to pull? Abby's at school. Go away and leave me alone!"

"Mom," Abigail tried once more.

"Help!" Nadine's cry was amazingly strong. "Somebody help me; I'm being attacked!"

Abigail backed away from the bed, her eyes misting. "Okay, Mom, I'm going." Abigail could never anticipate what Nadine's reaction to her would be. At times she was almost friendly, the way a normal person would respond to a pleasant stranger; other times were like today. But no matter how often it happened, or how convincingly Abigail reminded herself that it was the illness that prompted Nadine's bizarre behavior, her mother's rejection was always devastating. Again Abigail wondered why she continued to put herself through this torture. Surely her time would be better spent serving those with whom she could make a difference.

As she passed the lineup of wheelchairs along the way to the front entrance, shriveled hands reached out to her, and pleas of "Help me" accelerated her departure. She knew these people presented no danger to her, yet she was afraid. Perhaps it was the dread of her own possible decline into a similar snake pit of revulsion that prompted her feelings of repugnance. It was all such a waste! Why must these distorted specimens of human existence linger on, when their futures promised only endless misery? What was the purpose of it all? And would she someday join their ranks? With a sinking heart she made her way to the parking lot and climbed into her Toyota, checked her mascara in the visor mirror, and headed for work.

CHAPTER 2 - *Wednesday, December 15ᵗʰ*

Though Abigail loved her job, she often envied Tracey her stay-at-home status. Not that Tracey ever stayed at home! She could find more errands to run, more friends to visit, more stores to shop than any ten people had a right to. Abigail smiled and shook her head at the mental image of her sister flitting about from one endeavor to another.

Tracey was one of the fortunate minority who were everlastingly young, while Abigail aged with the rest of society. She humphed to herself; it felt like she'd been born old. She couldn't remember a time when she hadn't felt responsible for the welfare of the world. No matter what the scenario, it seemed she was always the one in charge, often because no one else was willing to step up to the plate, but just as often because "in charge" was where she felt most comfortable. Occasionally she'd vow to hold back, let someone else take over for a change, but her instinctive need for perfection could only be subjugated until the first inevitable lapse in judgment or performance. Then it was good old Abigail to the rescue.

Still, she had made her own decisions, chosen her own vocational path. Except for one brief interlude during the early years of her marriage, it had never been totally necessary for her to supplement the family income. Following that solitary rough patch, they could have managed on Barry's salary alone, if she'd ever been satisfied with less than the best, the way Tracey seemed to be. But "average" was not her style; she harbored an innate need to do more than merely scrape by. It was natural, she reasoned, to want a few privileges for your family: a good education for your children, music lessons, cultural exposure, and a decent style of living. It was also just possible that her need for a certain degree of luxury was the latent fruit born of the barren money tree that had, for so many years, graced her parents' domestic orchard.

Abigail got her first real job when she was barely sixteen, working in a restaurant. Her parents were scarcely able, at that time, to provide the most basic of necessities for their children, and that simply wasn't enough for their oldest daughter. Meese and Tracey had always been the charming ones: the cheerleaders, and the prom queens. She, herself, had never really felt like anyone special, and wanted the confidence which she believed that nice clothes and a little bit of cash would give her.

Thoughts of her sisters' popularity called to mind the time that Tracey was elected Sophomore Homecoming Princess. The results of the contest were to be kept secret until the assembly which was held on Friday morning to kick off the rest of the weekend's activities.

After all of the hullabaloo was over, their mom told them what had gone on behind the scenes. She'd received a phone call on Thursday afternoon, about five o'clock, informing her of Tracey's victory, and requesting that she secretly bring a formal dress to school the next morning for her daughter to wear after she was crowned. Tracey didn't own a formal, Nadine couldn't afford to buy one, and the fabric stores closed in an hour! On top of it all, Nadine had a meeting that night, starting at seven, which she couldn't miss, since she was in charge of the class, and responsible for presenting the lesson.

In a total panic she snatched her purse and ran to town, quickly found a pattern, grabbed some material, and rushed home just in time to leave for her appointment. After teaching her class she hurried back to the house, and while her three girls were at the homecoming bonfires, pulled out the sewing machine and began her project, her mind in a dither, and her fingers flying.

Just before midnight she dispatched Melvin to the high school to retrieve their daughters; then, when she subsequently heard the car pull back into the driveway, she tossed everything into the closet, and shut the door, just as her girls came bursting into the room. Nadine, feeling like her hand was in the cookie jar, greeted her daughters with a guilty smile. "How were the bonfires?"

"They were fun," Meese affirmed.

"Everyone was there," Tracey added.

Nadine listened as they expounded on the activity, then reminded them that they had school the next day, and sent them off to bed. The next morning, as soon as everyone was out the door, she pulled the partially finished garment from its hiding place, and sat again at the machine. A couple of hours later the project was finished and on its way to delivery–Melvin had already made one trip to school that morning to drop off the girls, but graciously offered to do it again, this time with dress in hand; Nadine could only hope it would fit.

Meanwhile, at the high school assembly, Tracey was standing on the stage in abject misery, anticipating her embarrassment when the whole school discovered that she didn't own a formal. Abigail and Meese, themselves, were suffering vicariously for their sister, not knowing of their mother's subterfuge, and sure that poor Tracey would soon be humiliated.

Abigail now smiled to herself. What a surprise they'd all had, and what a happy ending when Tracey's brand new shimmery blue gown was brought on stage and given to her. When they got home from school that day, Nadine apologized for the fact that she couldn't afford to include some appropriate shoes–all Tracey owned were a pair of clunky black jobs that she wore every day–but Tracey had been so amazed and relieved at the appearance of the dress, her shoes were of little concern.

Yes, Meese and Tracey were the popular ones, while Abigail and her older brother Jimmy were the "brains" in the family. She now chuckled over another memory that suddenly emerged. Jimmy's high school record, in spite of his intelligence, had been less than stellar. Mom had done her best to help and encourage him, but hadn't really pushed very hard, thinking that the poor kid was mentally deficient. After he finally got into college and his true colors were revealed, Mom confronted him one day, asking, "Why did you only make Cs and Ds in high school, when you're getting straight As in college?" He had grinned good-naturedly. "Mom, I was too smart to do all that stupid work!"

In spite of the fact that her sisters seemed to be having a lot more fun, Abigail had been reasonably content throughout her school years with concentrating on flawless behavior and excellent grades. But, at the beginning of her junior year in high school, she determined that she would break out of her mold, borrow a page from her sisters' book, and try out for the cheerleading squad. She faithfully attended each training session, learned–to perfection–all of the routines and songs, and then, at the last minute, chickened out, foreseeing the degradation of defeat. She knew she had the ability to perform as well as any of the other girls, but also realized that, no matter how good she was, it would be the popular ones who ended up with the pom poms.

She may have missed out on a few frivolities along the way, but her work and study ethics had done well by her. She'd attended an accredited university on a scholastic scholarship, landed a position with a prestigious civil engineering firm right out of college, and had been climbing the ladder of success ever since. Two years after graduation, she'd met her soul mate, a young man who was her equal in obsessing over the attainment of high goals. They were married five months later, and had enjoyed a compatible relationship ever since. There'd thankfully been no regrets about that particular choice.

Abigail sighed. She knew that, at this point, she could retire any time she desired. Her children were grown and married. She had a beautiful home, a new car, and money in the bank. Barry had in place a good retirement plan, which, when the time came, would undoubtedly be more than adequate to sustain them. It was also a fact that, as their ages increased, their wants and needs diminished. But her career had become a way of life by now. Without it, she didn't know how she would occupy her time. Idle and bored were also not her style.

Her excuse, to herself as well as others, was that someone had to subsidize her father's Social Security income; it simply wasn't enough to pay his bills. And, even though the exorbitant fees charged for her mother's care were paid by Social Security and Medicaid, there would undoubtedly be a funeral—or two—in the not too distant future, and they didn't come cheap. So, for the time being at least, she would proceed to play the eight-to-five game.

Still, Abigail's long ago choices continued to trouble her throughout the day. Had she allowed her priorities to become skewed? Should she have given her children fewer advantages, and more of her time?

Would they have been happier, better adjusted? What if she someday ended up like her mother, her only memories of her offspring being those of their early childhood, the time they had spent in daycare? And, finally, when the fat lady sang, how important would have been her vocational success? She sighed. Well, the die had been cast many years before; it was too late now to begin questioning her judgment.

Again she was reminded of her early morning visit to the center, and the strange encounter with her mother's nurse. She'd have to talk to Tracey as soon as she returned home that evening, run the whole thing by her, and see what she thought. Meanwhile, she had arrived at her office, and needed to redirect her energies to the workload waiting on her desk.

The day proceeded with no unforeseen problems, and at five-thirty, when she turned the key in the lock on her front door, the phone was ringing. Her sister had beat her to the punch. "I'm trying to plan Christmas dinner," Tracey said, "and need to know how many will be here. Are both your kids going to make it?"

"As far as I know. Rachel and Mark will be going to his parents' house that morning, but promised to be at your place in time for dinner. Paul's family plan to come here and follow us over. What about your gang? Will they all be there?"

"Yeah. One of us will have to go to the airport to pick up Alan about noon. The other two will be here en masse. So take some Valium and wear your earplugs."

Abigail laughed. "Your little grandkids aren't that bad."

"I didn't say they were bad, just high spirited, demanding, noisy, and destructive."

"Tracey," Abigail's tone became plaintive, "I need to ask you something. Have any of the nurses at the care center mentioned anything to you about Mom having occasional moments of clarity?"

Tracey snorted. "Mom? No. Why?"

"I stopped by this morning on my way to work, and the night nurse was just leaving. She claimed that she and Mom had talked, and that Mom had even described me to her. Do you think it's possible?"

"Sounds to me like that nurse was snitching a few meds on the side."

"But she knew my name!" countered Abigail. "She called me 'Abby,' like Mom always does."

"I'm sure our names are listed in Mom's paper work."

"As Abigail, not Abby. I haven't been Abby since I was twelve," Abigail protested. "Well, except to the family, to whom I will never be *more* than twelve."

"Still, it's not a huge leap. Anyway, I'm going over there tomorrow. I'll ask, but I wouldn't get my hopes up. Even if Mom did seem to come around for awhile, it was probably just a fluke."

Abigail returned the handset to its base, and sat mulling over the strange events of the morning. She drew a deep breath, and puffed out her cheeks. "Tracey's probably right; I shouldn't get my hopes up."

"You talking to me, Ab?" Barry called out from his office.

"No, just to the little voices in my head."

"And are your little voices telling you anything I want to hear?"

Abigail laid her coat across the back of a kitchen chair and walked down the hall toward the sound of her husband's voice. "Probably, but we'll talk about it later. How about you?" she asked as she entered the plushly furnished room. "Anything out of the ordinary going on?"

Barry gave her a quick kiss. "Same-ol; I have some spread sheets I need to go through tonight."

She turned to leave. "I'll call you when dinner's ready. Are soup and sandwiches okay?"

"Whatever."

As they shared the simple meal, Abigail told of her experience with the nurse at the care center, but Barry gave little credence to her concerns. "Are you sure you didn't misunderstand?"

"What was to misunderstand? She called me by name, told me that she and Mom had been talking, and acted completely nonchalant about the whole thing."

"That's why it seems a little incredible. If your mom had actually had a breakthrough, don't you think it would have engendered a little more excitement?"

"I don't know, Barry." Abigail's tone was a mite testy. "I'm just telling you what happened."

Barry swiped his fingers through his hair, hardly daring to make his next suggestion. He threw a pensive glance at his wife, then dropped his eyes back to his plate.

"What!" demanded Abigail.

"You've been under a lot of stress lately, with your parents and your job. Is it possible that you dreamed it?"

"Barry," she snapped, "I do know the difference between reality and fantasy."

He shrugged. "Then is it possible that she wasn't really a nurse? Maybe one of the residents was playing make-believe."

Abigail slumped as the breath whooshed out of her lungs. "Be real, Barry. You know very well they don't have a psych ward there."

Barry chortled. "Hon, the whole place is a psych ward!"

Abigail couldn't help but smile. "Anyway, this was a young woman; she didn't look more than twenty-five."

"Then the only other explanation I can think of is that the nurse is maybe half a bubble off plumb."

"But she seemed so—"

Barry stood and brushed the crumbs from his lap. "I don't know, Hon. I wish I had some answers for you, but right now I need to get busy; I have a ton of work to do." With that, he exited the kitchen, leaving his wife with her thoughts in turmoil.

She cleaned up the kitchen, folded some laundry and put it away, then watched a Christmas show on TV. When she finally crawled into bed, she was still puzzling over the morning's encounter, and no closer to an explanation.

Ten miles away, at the care center, Nadine stirred in her sleep and slowly opened her eyes. "You're here," she whispered, as if speaking too loudly might shatter the image beside her.

"Didn't I tell you I would be?" Lisa gently chided. "You feel like talking for awhile?"

"You don't mind listening to an old woman ramble?"

Lisa giggled. "That's part of my job description." She fussed with the bed and the pillows until Nadine was settled comfortably, then again sat in a chair at her side. "I'd like to hear more about your family."

Nadine was pleased. Nothing made her happier than telling her stories. "Jimmy is my oldest, then Abby, Meese and Tracey. Long after we thought we were through, Danny came along. I have to say I wasn't real happy when I found out I was pregnant at age forty-two. Tracey, my baby, was nineteen, and after that many years, I wasn't sure I was up to the task, physically or emotionally. It was hard to imagine myself once again packing around an infant, taking him everywhere with me. I was so out of practice I was afraid I might forget and leave him somewhere. And I wasn't at all sure that I could again become a member of the league of women breast-feeders."

Lisa chuckled. "But you must have managed."

"We do what we have to do, I guess. Our bodies seem to adapt, even when they're middle-aged. And Danny was a joy: a red-headed, freckle-faced, mischievous, rowdy joy. Even though his sibs were grown, and he was pretty much an only child, I don't believe he was ever bored. He helped with the farm chores, and was active in sports. When he wasn't milking the cow, or feeding the pigs, or playing football, or wrestling, he liked to tube down the irrigation canal, and ride the horses. When he was little, he used to swing through the branches of the trees behind our house, pretending he was Tarzan. He could always find something to keep himself occupied." Nadine shook her head. "I wasn't always aware of where he was or what he was up to; I just know that he was never one of those kids who hung around the house, complaining because there wasn't anything to do.

"Even as an infant he was able to entertain himself. That's not to say he wasn't a handful. I remember once at church, when Danny was about a year old. My husband must have been one of the speakers or something, because he had to sit on the stand, so I was by myself in the congregation with Danny. I can't recall that he was doing anything out of the ordinary, just being his usual boisterous self. Well, about half way through the meeting I was so fed up with his antics I marched up to the podium, plunked Danny down in my husband's lap, and marched back to my seat. I heard a few chuckles from the congregation, but I'm sure that most of the mothers there understood perfectly."

They both laughed at the image this brought to mind, and Nadine went on, "That reminds me of the story about the little boy who was acting up in church, so his obviously irritated dad picked him up and started to carry him out. The little boy, at this point, knew he was in trouble, and began screaming, 'Bishop! Help!'"

Lisa laughed again, a charming, tinkly-toned sound that warmed Nadine's heart. "It's very gratifying, telling my stories to such an appreciative audience," she said, "so you'll have to tell me when you get tired of listening, because I could go on forever."

Lisa smiled. "And I think I could listen forever, so don't stop now."

Nadine nodded. "Good answer! So, where was I?" She paused, fetching the remnants of her thoughts, then resumed her narrative. "One day, when Danny was about two, he was riding with me in the car, and experimentally pulled on his door handle just as I began a left turn. From the corner of my eye I observed as the door flew open, and Danny took a nose dive onto the gravel road. Slamming on the brakes and flinging myself across the seat, I seized his coat-tail, thus dragging his face along in the dirt. Of course, by this time I was frantic, and I couldn't figure out why the car was still moving forward, until I realized that, in my effort to reach Danny, my foot had come off of the brake pedal. With a burst of effort I once again applied the brakes and hauled him inside. His lip was split wide open and his face abraded, but he was alive, and I wanted to weep with relief. I don't think he even cried, just sat there stunned and bleeding. So, instead of going to the store, as planned, we went directly to the hospital, and then, on the way home, I became traumatized, thinking about what might have been. If I hadn't grabbed him when I did, the back tire would probably have run him over." Nadine gave a compulsive shiver. "It still makes me shudder to think of it.

"Danny wore a faint scar on his upper lip from then on, but it didn't hurt his looks any. He was a handsome young man, very popular in high

29

school, especially with the girls. I think he had dates with three different young women for graduation night. How he managed that I don't know; I didn't even ask.

"Whenever I think about high school graduations, I think of the time when Tracey was a baby, and I attended the graduation of one of my nieces. It was held in the high school gym, and because my baby was strictly on mothers' milk, I took her along, sat in the bleachers and, to keep her quiet, nursed her throughout the entire ceremony." Nadine chortled and shook her head. "A young man sitting next to me was captivated by my little daughter, and spent much of the time ogling her, trying to get a better look. He didn't realize that she was having a very prolonged meal, and probably wondered why I refused to uncover her face and show her off. I simply feigned an insouciant oblivion to his interest, and pretended to be totally caught up in the speeches being presented.

"I also took Tracey along to my softball games that summer, and fed her between running bases and performing my duties as catcher. I was determined that she would never be bottle-fed, so, while Melvin often tended the other children, Tracey was my constant companion.

"When my three girls were little, they were almost identical in appearance, and since there wasn't much more than two years between the oldest and youngest, I always dressed them to match: three little peas from the same pod. I was so proud of them." She hiked her eyebrows. "Still am."

Nadine smiled as another memory took shape. "For most of their childhood they had to share a bed, and I remember one morning, when they were about five, six and seven. I went to wake them, and was particularly struck by the similarity of their appearance. After they got up, I told them, 'You girls looked so much alike, I didn't know which one was which.' Tracey got this look on her face like, 'well, duh,' and said, 'You should have looked in our mouths, and if there were no teeth, it was me!' Nadine chuckled. "She always did have the most interesting take on things.

"When they were teenagers, people often mistook them for triplets. Oh, they didn't wear matching outfits any more, but they still maintained a strong resemblance to one another. Strangers on the street would stop to notice them, and it took some time even for their school friends to tell them apart."

"I'll bet that was fun for them," remarked Lisa.

Nadine nodded. "Oh, yes, they had a great time fooling the boys. It wasn't long, though, before each one began to expand into her own unique individuality. When Meese reached five-one, and ninety-five pounds, that was about as far as she got, while the other two kept sprouting upward. They've both remained slim, a condition I never was able to achieve; they got their skinny genes from their dad. And, while Meese's strawberry locks never changed, Abby's hair began to turn darker, and Tracey chose to help along the blonde in hers (I'm sure that's still the case).   "Abby became my worrier; she always needs her ducks in a row. Meese was the peacemaker, and Tracey–she just wanted to have fun (I think that's also still the case). But, no matter how my girls' appearances and personalities changed, their comradery never wavered. They were sisters, through and through."

Nadine's gaze turned inward, and Lisa allowed her time to ruminate momentarily before commenting, "They were lucky to have each other."

Nadine started slightly, as if suddenly catapulted into the present. "Yes, they were. As I've noticed other families over the years, I've realized how blessed I am to have children who care for each other, who are able to get along, and who have maintained their integrity. Even Tracey, with her rugged history, has managed to put her feet back on solid ground. No thanks to me, mind you. I think I've made every mistake in the book, when it comes to my kids."

"Maybe you're too hard on yourself. You've just told me that your children are upstanding, caring adults. What more do you want?"

Nadine only had to think for a moment. "A family portrait."

"Excuse me?"

"Crazy, huh," Nadine admitted. "I used to look at all these huge pictures hanging on people's walls, with their whole clan around them, and I would think, 'My family knew how much I wanted one of those; why didn't they care enough to see that it happened?' It was important to me because of what it represented: a strong, united family. Perhaps I thought that, with all of us stuck together in a picture, nothing could ever tear us apart. Stupid, maybe, but I still cry over the fact that that picture never got taken." The tear that appeared on Nadine's cheek at that moment attested to the truth of her confession.

"I'm truly sorry," sympathized Lisa. "But you may be wrong. Maybe your family didn't really know how badly you wanted it."

Nadine shook her head sadly. "They knew."

"Well, it isn't too late; with the photographic technology of today, they could still make it happen. A photographer could use an old photo of Meese and add it in." Lisa offered.

"Wouldn't be the same," mourned Nadine.

"Let me see if I can figure something out; you may be more pleased than you think with the result. So, meanwhile, tell me more good things about your children."

Nadine smiled. "They weren't exactly little angels. With my four oldest ones so close together, there was always some sort of mischief afoot. One day, shortly after Abby began to crawl, I left her in the house with her big–but not very big–brother while I went outside to hang diapers on the line. As I was heading back inside, I heard Abby crying rather vociferously. When I entered the kitchen I found her sitting on the floor, face upturned, with Jimmy shaking pepper into her eyes."

"Ooh!" gasped Lisa. "Did it cause any damage?"

"Only a mild heart attack . . . mine!

"Then, when Jimmy was about three, my parents took a trip to Utah, and my mom sent him a little plastic bear filled with honey. His appetite immediately increased a hundred-fold. It was so much fun squeezing the honey from the bear's head, it became the seasoning for every meal. He swirled it into his soup, put it on his eggs, had it with cottage cheese, and even on cantaloupe.

"Yuck!"

"Yes, indeed. And that brings me to the point of the story. The washing machine that we owned when Tracey was a toddler had a drain hose that emptied into the laundry tub on the back porch. For some reason Jimmy thought it would be a good idea to put the plug into the drain before I did the washing. Well, you can guess what happened! So, while I was cleaning up the flood, Abby took Jimmy's plastic honey bear from the kitchen table and decorated my bedspread, while Tracey found a box of Ritz crackers, which had inadvertently been left within her reach, and was smashing them into the carpet. Meanwhile, Meese got hold of my pattern tracing wheel and punched little holes all over our new coffee table. Well, when I say 'new'–it probably came from the thrift store, but it was new to us. I can appreciate, now, the humor in all of their mischief, but on that day I just plopped down in the middle of the floor, and cried.

"Then there was the time that Jimmy's pet rabbit had babies. He was the first to discover them, so carried each of the brand new bunnies into the house and put them into the desk drawers, then covered them up with his toys, nice and cozy. Fortunately, he then came and told me how well he'd taken care of them. Only one died."

By now Lisa was laughing delightedly, and Nadine couldn't help but join in. "It wasn't so funny at the time," she protested, "but that was pretty indicative of my day to day experience for those first few years.

"When Tracey was less than a year old, my husband Melvin lost his job. Until that time, we had been living in California, but decided that that would the opportune time to move to Utah, where Melvin could continue his schooling. His brother owned a neighborhood grocery store in Malad, Idaho, and helped us out by offering Melvin a temporary position until we got settled somewhere. Therefore, it was decided that he would go to Idaho, while I stayed behind with the children, and saw to the selling of our house. Then we would meet in Utah, find a place to live, and get Melvin enrolled at the university, while both of us looked for part-time jobs. That, of course, meant that I eventually had to make the trip to our Utah location on my own, with only my children as traveling companions.

"I talked my girlfriend Sharon into accompanying me; her parents lived in Salt Lake City, and were anxious for her to visit. She also had a few small children who would necessarily come along. My parents helped me pack up a rented U-haul trailer, and then reluctantly waved us on our way. My mom told me later how difficult that had been for her, watching us pull away, loaded to the hilt with kids and furniture, but I saw it as a great adventure.

"When we pulled into Provo, after twenty-three straight hours on the road, Sharon said she couldn't see my eyes any more; they were swollen shut. Her parents met us there on 500 West, and took her and her brood home with them, and I checked into a motel with my four little ones.

"Not only was I exhausted, but we were all starving, so I put the children to bed with strict instructions to stay put while I went across the street to buy some sandwiches. I'd no sooner opened the door to the café than I heard Jimmy hollering from across the way that Meese had crawled out of bed. I ran back to the motel, settled Meese down, and crossed the street once more. The minute I reached my destination, I again heard a distressed cry from the motel. This time Jimmy had to go potty. I ran back, assisted him, tucked the children in one more time, and finally was able to complete my mission. I don't remember ever being so tired!

"Melvin came down from Idaho the next morning so we could look for a place to live, and a few hours later we were moving our scanty belongings into a duplex."

"But Melvin didn't have a job yet," Lisa commented.

"No. We were young and invincible. It never occurred to us that things might not work out. Fortunately, we had friends in Provo who were beginning construction on a new house, and offered Melvin some work hammering nails. I was hired on as a sales clerk at J.C. Penney, working the evening shift. We somehow made do."

"Did you ever go hungry?"

Nadine shook her head. "Never in our lives did we go without the essentials. There were times, over the years, when I thought we couldn't possibly make it, but something always turned up. The Lord took care of us. He always has." She yawned.

"You're getting sleepy," Lisa observed. "Why don't we continue this tomorrow night?"

"You'll be sure to come back?" Nadine worried.

"I promise." Lisa lowered the bed and leaned over to kiss Nadine's wrinkled cheek. "Sleep tight. Don't let the bed bugs bite."

Nadine smiled sleepily. "That's what I used to say to my children." She closed her eyes then, and didn't hear Lisa's quietly murmured, "I know."

CHAPTER 3 - *Thursday, December 16th*

After breakfast the following morning Tracey fished her coat from the entry closet, grabbed her purse and keys and hopped into her clunker of a Hyundai. Her visits to the care center were generally less traumatic than her sister's. Abigail always took matters too seriously. Things were what they were, and constantly bemoaning the fact only made them worse.

Tracey planned to check out Abigail's story, but was quite sure that her sister's understanding of the other night's events was merely due to some kind of mis-communication. Nadine had been in a fog for the past three years, and, as far as Tracey knew, it was impenetrable. She couldn't imagine what the nurse's motive would be for whitewashing the situation if, indeed, she had actually done so. The most logical explanation, as atypical as it may be, was that Abigail had totally misconstrued her meaning.

Tracey pulled into the parking lot and entered the facility. "Is the administrator available this morning?" she asked the receptionist.

"I'll page her, if you'd like to have a seat."

Tracey chose to stand and pace, as if that might speed along the woman's appearance. It was not a long wait; five minutes later Miss

Wills rounded the corner. She was dressed in a gray business suit, carried a clipboard, and resembled nothing more than a middle aged schoolmarm, complete with tidy bun at the back of her neck, reading glasses dangling from a chain, resting on her ample bosom–and attitude. She greeted Tracey coolly and invited her into the office. "What can I do for you?" she asked, as she seated herself behind the large desk and motioned for Tracey to take a chair opposite.

"It's about my mom, Nadine," Tracey elucidated, as she accepted the woman's gestured invitation. "One of the nurses told my sister that Mom was alert and coherent the night before last, and I just wondered if it's really possible for that to happen."

Miss Wills, with all the acidic propriety incumbent upon a woman in her elevated position, smiled indulgently. "Sometimes patients with dementia can seem relatively normal for short periods of time, although their minds are never really clear. As advanced as your mother's condition is, it's very unlikely that any kind of meaningful communication occurred. But I can speak with the nurse, if you'd like. Which one was it?"

Tracey pursed her lips. "I don't know her name. Abigail just said it was the nurse who worked two nights ago. She purportedly had a long talk with my mom."

Miss Wills tucked an errant gray hair behind one ear, lifted a single eyebrow, and gave Tracey a look that was clearly patronizing. She sighed. "I'll have to check the charts then. I'll get in touch with you when I have ascertained the validity–or error–of your sister's report."

Tracey came that close to rolling her eyes, and had to clamp her lips closed to squelch the rebuff that begged utterance. Better to not antagonize the *help* (she almost smirked in silent revenge as she mentally affixed the appellation to the grande dame wannabe). With applaudable self restraint she stood, offered a curt, "I'll wait to hear from you," and left to find her mother.

Nadine was slumped over in her wheelchair, parked in front of the west wing nurse's station. "Mom?" Tracey took her hand and squeezed it.

Nadine's head popped up. "I need to go home now."

"This is your home, Mom."

"In a pig's eye! This is a stinkin' looney bin. I gotta get out of here. Can you take me home?"

Tracey had long ago learned the futility of fruitless reasoning or argument; her mother only became increasingly agitated and hostile. Tracey's best ploy was distraction, so she delved the depths of her shoulder bag and pulled out the one thing she knew would capture her mother's fleeting interest. "Here, I brought you a Hershey bar."

Nadine eyed her daughter suspiciously. "Does it have almonds?"

Tracey smiled. "Would I bring any other kind?"

Nadine grabbed the chocolate and ripped open the wrapper. "I need a drink of water. Can't eat a Hershey bar without water."

"Okay, Mom, wait here while I get you one."

"Hmph!" snorted Nadine. "And just where do you think I might go?"

"Now that's hard to say," Tracey teased. "I just don't want to come back, and find out that you've called a cab and gone shopping."

Nadine chortled. "I've got the time, if you've got the dime."

Tracey's eyes blinked in astonishment. That was a blast from the past. Many a time, as a pre-teen, she'd begged her mother to take her to the store to purchase some fashion item that "everybody" was wearing. More often than not, her mother's reply was the same as she'd just uttered. There had never been enough cash to indulge in unnecessary fripperies. "Fashion" had to wait until Tracey was earning her own money. With a glimmer of hope at hearing again her mom's well-worn phrase, she asked, "Mom, do you remember how many times you used to tell me that?"

Nadine squinted at her daughter. "Who *are* you?"

"I'm Tracey, Mom, your youngest daughter."

Nadine leaned forward and, with a scowl, studied the face before her. "Tracey? What are you doing here? You should be in school."

Tracey gave her mother a rueful smile. "I haven't been in school for years, Mom."

Nadine looked puzzled. "Have you been playing hooky? You know how I feel about that."

Tracey sighed. "I'll go get you a glass of water, Mom, so you can eat your Hershey bar."

Nadine looked down at the forgotten candy in her hand, smiled at the discovery, and brought the delicious confection to her mouth. She took a bite and chewed slowly, savoring each morsel, until her daughter returned, then declared, "I have to start lunch now; will you get the table set?"

"Sure, Mom." Tracey handed her the glass, and kissed her lightly on the forehead. "But then I have to leave. I'll be back in a couple of days."

"Will you bring more candy?"

Tracey smiled. "You can count on it. Chocolate? Or do you want something different?" But Nadine's attention span had already hit its limit. She was making quick work of the Hershey bar, running her tongue into the corners of her mouth to retrieve any tidbits that attempted escape. Tracey shrugged. "See you later, then."

Tracey made her way down the hall, her three inch heels clicking on the tiled floor. "Hi, Mabel," she greeted a bent figure in one of the wheelchairs which lined the walls. "I see you've got your pretty blue dress on." Mabel's eyes remained downcast, acknowledging neither the salutation nor the compliment, and Tracey continued on her way. "Henry, you behave yourself today. No more flirting with the nurses!" Henry's toothless mouth opened wide in a silent belly laugh, and Tracey patted his shoulder as she passed. "Robert, you been fishing lately?"

Robert grinned broadly. "You shoulda seen the one that got away." He spread his arms wide. "It was this big!"

"Ah, Robert, you know where you go when you tell whoppers like that, don't you?"

"Sure do. Fish heaven!" It was their customary little joke, rehearsed at each of Tracey's visits, and subsequently repeated by Robert to his fellow inpatients several times throughout the day.

Tracey raised her arm in a final salute and pushed her way through the front doors. It was beginning to snow, and she pulled her coat closer around her, then stood, gazing upward, as the soft flakes fell weightlessly upon her shoulders. She loved the first snowfall of the season, and this year it had been late in coming. Breathing in deeply, she filled her nostrils with its unique fragrance, and prayed silently that she'd never find herself in a place where she'd be deprived of this simple luxury.

In reminiscence of childhood pleasures, she closed her eyes and opened her mouth, letting the delicate crystals float inside to melt on her tongue. She almost giggled with pleasure, less from the sensation than from the long-ago memories it evoked: tubing with her brother and sisters down the hill behind their house, sleigh rides in the back of a farm wagon with a dozen or so other teenagers, all of them freezing, yet never feeling the cold, Christmas caroling to the neighborhood widows and shut-ins.

There had been a good many snowfalls since then, along with a multitude of memories in the making, not all of which were as pleasant as those from her childhood. Her life had not exactly been one of sweetness and light. After graduating from high school she'd wanted to strike out on her own. Not quite eighteen, she'd immediately secured a fairly decent job, and shortly thereafter moved into an apartment with a girl she'd met through mutual friends. A few days later, while Tracey was at work, her roommate moved out, taking with her all of Tracey's belongings, as well as the groceries, and the deposit money Tracey had paid in order to move in. Too embarrassed to call her parents, and with nowhere else to go, Tracey had slept under a tree for a week, and then stayed with a friend for a couple of days, until a male coworker volunteered to put a roof over her head, the only hitch being that his own head would be under that same roof.

Desperate, she had accepted his offer, moved in, and soon become embroiled in a disastrous relationship. Then, finding herself pregnant, she had opted out of the expected wedding, even though the boy was willing. At some level, she had known all along that what she felt for him was not love, so rather than continue the farce, she'd chosen to raise her child on her own. It was at that point that she swallowed her pride, moved back home, and availed herself of her parents' financial and emotional support.

Not many months after her son Alan's birth, when a succeeding brief romance resulted in yet another pregnancy, she had given up for adoption a beautiful baby daughter. Receiving no counsel, one way or the other, from her mom and dad–it had to be her own decision–the choice she made had, at the time, seemed the best alternative, the most advantageous for the child, even though her own heart was broken. Nevertheless, she would always wonder if anyone else could love her little girl the way she did, and the doubt had forever torn her to shreds.

It wasn't long before she met someone who seemed to be the man of her dreams. They were soon married, but she should have realized when he showed up late for the wedding–he'd stopped on the way for a round of golf with his buddies–that there might be limits to his commitment. Five years, another baby girl, and countless affairs later (his, not hers), she divorced him and was, once again, on her own, this time with two children for whom she alone must provide. Years of trauma and heartache were hers before she finally found her present husband Dale. Though he had proved to be a balm to her bleeding soul, not even he knew the whole story of her struggle. There were things she, herself, wanted to forget.

Alan and Jaimee, her two reasons for living, had had differing opinions about gaining a new father. Jaimee was all for it, but Alan considered himself to be the man of the house, and saw no need to bring in an interloper. For that, and other reasons, Tracey's determination to marry again was a long time in coming.

She'd finally reached a point in her career when she no longer needed financial subsidy, and considering her past failed relationships, she was way beyond gun shy. If Dale hadn't been so persistent–one of the things she loved about him–she'd probably still be single. And, of course, Tyler would still be living with the angels, awaiting his turn on earth. She smiled as thoughts of her youngest son played across her mind, the reward for her years of sticking it out through all of the hard work and travail.

Well, she couldn't stand here all day. She and Jaimee were going Christmas shopping after lunch, and she had some sewing she wanted to finish before they left. She climbed into the car, turned the key, and waited for the old machine to grind into life. Finally, when the motor began to rumble, she patted the dashboard. "Atta girl, Tallulah." As she backed out of the parking space, a car with a young man behind the wheel came barreling around the corner behind her. Slamming on his brakes, the driver scowled as he flipped an obscene gesture in her direction. Tracey put on a huge grin, rolled down her window, leaned out and waved happily, calling a "Merry Christmas," and leaving the befuddled young man wondering if she was–heaven forbid–a friend of his mother's.

The afternoon with her daughter was well spent; Jaimee made a considerable dent in her shopping list, and Tracey finished up everyone on hers except for her husband Dale. He was always a hard case. Last year the two of them had simply gone out together and chosen for themselves; that seemed to be the easiest solution, though possibly not the most satisfying.

Her other yearly dilemma was her father. He was at the age when he didn't need or want anything, which made gift giving a frustrating challenge. Lately she had discovered what she'd initially regarded as well-thought-out presents, from earlier Christmases, stashed away, still in their boxes, amid the life-long accumulation that cluttered his garage.

Today, however, she'd managed, with Jaimee's help, to find what she considered the perfect gift: an electric apple peeler. Nadine and the children used to tease him about his penchant for that particular fruit, as well as his aversion to eating its most nutritious part. Now he no longer had the patience to pare the apples with a knife, so seldom indulged his former addiction. It was a simple gift, but one she optimistically hoped he'd appreciate.

After dinner Tracey wrapped the day's purchases, watched her favorite television show–it was Dale's bowling night with his buddies—and fell, exhausted, into bed, pleased with the day's accomplishments, but once again contemplating Abigail's strange assertions concerning their mother. It wasn't like her sister to be confused; Abby had always been the one who was quick to comprehend. Many a time she'd corrected Tracey about her own false assumptions, but the shoe had never before been on the other foot.

Tracey smiled, considering how often Abby had rescued her from difficult situations. In grammar school Tracey'd been kind of a gawky looking kid, and that, combined with her penchant for always speaking her mind, gave rise to many a childish brawl, with big sister forever coming to her aid. She was a force to be reckoned with, and took good care of her younger siblings. But, when it came to their mom, even Abigail was now helpless to save. Tracey drifted off to sleep, still puzzled, but assuring herself that the riddle would surely be solved on the following day.

"Nadine, it's time for your meds." The nurse shook her gently.

"Where's Lisa?" was the angry reply.

"You've been having a dream, Dear, but you need to take your meds now."

Nadine begrudgingly accepted the little green pills and swallowed them down with a sip of water. Then, after churlishly pulling a face at the nurse, she turned her back and pulled the covers over her head. "Sweet dreams," the nurse sang out sarcastically as she left.

The old woman dozed lightly as she awaited the best part of each night. It wasn't long before the door opened again, rousing her. She then lowered the blanket just enough to reveal two distrustful eyes. Her brow quickly cleared. "Oh, it's you."

"How are you feeling?" inquired Lisa.

"Better now. I was afraid you weren't coming."

"No worries. I'm a woman of my word." She went about her usual routine of fluffing pillows, straightening bed covers, and drawing up a chair for their ensuing conversation. "Do you need anything?"

"No, I'm fine."

"Are you comfortable?" At Nadine's nod, she smiled and asked, "So, where did we leave off last night?"

"I think we had just moved to Provo." Nadine's lips slowly curved upward. "Physical fitness was then becoming a national pastime, and all of the young mothers on our street, including me, were joining the ranks. To miss our morning workout would have been tantamount to selling one of our children. As much as we'd have liked to, on occasion, we wouldn't have dared. It was a matter of conscience. One of the men in the neighborhood who worked nights and was home during the day, said he could always tell when it was time for Jack LaLanne's exercise program on TV. Up and down the street, at the exact same moment, all of the drapes closed." They both chuckled at the visual image.

"I always used to think that, by the time I reached a certain age, I wouldn't be concerned anymore with how I looked." Nadine grinned, "I just haven't reached that age yet. Although, to see me now," she grimaced, "you'd assume I was beyond caring. I never thought I'd see the day when I wouldn't comb my hair or put on makeup."

"You want to play 'Beauty Shop'?"

Nadine's eyes widened in surprise, and she gave a slight chortle. "My girls and I used to do that. They were always wanting to give me a make-over. I remember, when they were teenagers, the 'Afro' came into style. So we gave each other perms, and ratted our hair out to here." She lifted her hands to each side of her head, indicating the voluminous proportions of their coifs.

46

"I thought you might be in the mood tonight," grinned Lisa, "so I brought along some supplies."

Nadine's brow furrowed. "I must say, you're no ordinary nurse."

Lisa merely lifted a shoulder. "I'm pretty sure I can't create an Afro, but I can probably manage a French twist."

"Oh, my goodness, I wore a twist for years!" Nadine was delighted at the prospect, and felt a surge of energy course through her body. "What fun!"

"Let's get you out of bed and into the wheelchair, and then I'll do your hair while you put on some makeup."

Feeling almost like a pre-teen, about to play at her mother's dressing table, Nadine swung her legs to the side of the bed, and made the transfer, her body sitting erect with anticipation. Lisa brushed her hair away from her face, placed a few bobby pins to secure the back, and swirled the locks into the style which the old woman remembered so well. Meanwhile, Nadine held the mirror in her left hand while she contorted her facial muscles to facilitate the application of eyebrows, mascara, and lipstick. She then studied the resulting reflection. "A vast improvement, to be sure, but I still get a shock whenever I look into a mirror. When you're young you never really expect to get old. It comes as quite a surprise."

"Well, I think you look beautiful. Not a day over eighty!" Nadine endeavored to affect affront, but couldn't help laughing along with her young nurse. "How about you getting back into bed, and I'll polish your nails while you go on with what you were telling me." Nadine complied, and was soon settled against her pillows, her fingers spread out over the covers in readiness, while Lisa retrieved the coral polish from her pocket.

"You even brought the right color."

47

Lisa canted her head to one side. "You don't look like a 'pink' person. So I figured it had to be either coral or red. Red would be the conventional color for Christmas, but my guess is that you're the kind who likes to snub your nose at protocol." She gave Nadine a wink, and took her hand to begin the manicure. "You were telling me about your exercise program."

"Well, besides exercising, I was always on a diet of one kind or another: Mayo Clinic, Jenny Craig, Weight Watchers, Snacker's, Hot Dog, Cabbage Soup. You name it, I've starved through it. My friends used to laugh when I'd mention my 'Fudge Diet.' Need I say that I formulated it, myself? I'd explain to them, 'It's easy! You just make a batch of fudge, and then snarf the whole thing down in one sitting. It makes you so sick, you don't want to eat again for three days!'"

"And, did it work?"

"No. But it was popular."

Lisa giggled. "So did you keep on exercising as you got older?"

"Oh, yes. For a long time I taught aerobic dance. But, of course, that was years later. 'Aerobic' wasn't even a word in our vocabulary until the mid 1970s."

"And when was it that you lived in Provo?"

"The early 60s. We eventually were able to purchase a house, and I was ecstatic about having a home of our own. I could finally paint walls and hang pictures. The kids could have a swing, and maybe even a dog. Our neighbors would be farther away than just on the other side of a thin wall. Ah, heaven!

"Teenage twin girls lived next door and occasionally stayed with our little clan so Melvin and I could go out to dinner or to a show. It didn't happen often; we usually couldn't afford the price of a hamburger or movie admission, let alone the twenty-five cents an hour baby-sitting fee. But, once in awhile, we'd break loose.

"About that time, dancing styles were going through some dramatic changes, with the advent of the stomp and the mashed potatoes, among others. Melvin and I loved to dance, and I was determined to learn these new steps. They did not, however, come naturally to me. I invited one of the twins over one night–Melvin was working late–and asked her to teach me the 'moves.'

"We worked diligently–well, I worked; Elaine danced–for several hours before my young instructor had to go home. I then started up the phonograph again to practice on my own. Jimmy, who was six at the time, came into the room while I was rehearsing, stood watching for a few moments, and then placed his hands on his hips and chastised me thoroughly. 'What would Dad think if he saw you doing that?' he scolded. I have no idea what I was doing that was so offensive, but needless to say, that was the end of my modern dancing pursuits!"

"I don't get it," Lisa protested. "It wasn't suggestive, was it?"

"It wasn't supposed to be, but like I said, I wasn't exactly an adept student. Jimmy was obviously appalled. You wouldn't have thought him to be so easily scandalized, considering the fact that, when he was about two, he used to wait until I was occupied with something, and then go play in the middle of the street in his birthday suit. I often wondered if the neighbors thought he didn't have a mother." Nadine lifted her eyebrows and shrugged. "I guess, in the intervening four years, he'd matured to the point of piety.

"I spent a lot of time, in those days, at the emergency room. One or another of my children was always needing stitches. One morning I had them loaded into the car for a jaunt into town when I decided to make a quick trip to the potty. I told them to stay put, and then I hurried into the house. About five minutes later, upon emerging from the bathroom, I discovered my front hall filled with neighbors, one of whom was holding a bloody faced Abby in his arms. It seems that she had tired of sitting in the car, and decided to ride her tricycle while waiting for me. Just as she pedaled behind the back bumper, Meese disengaged the parking brake. The tire rolled over Abby's arm, removing the skin, and the bumper ripped a deep gash in her forehead, the scar of which still pops out when she's upset about something."

"That must have been frightening for you," Lisa observed.

"Well, of course I was scared, but she had remained conscious, so I didn't panic. I simply asked one of the women standing in my entry to watch the other children while I drove Abby to the emergency room. When we got in to see the doctor, they wanted to wrap her in what resembled a straight jacket—it was referred to as a 'papoose'—to tie her arms down, and keep her from thrashing about. Abby became hysterical, and I assumed it was the thought of being so strictly confined that had her terrified. Years later I learned that, when she heard the word 'papoose,' she concluded that they were going to turn her into an Indian."

Lisa hooted. "So what happened?"

"I finally talked the doctor into letting me hold her while he stitched. As soon as I took her in my arms, she quieted right down, and never made another peep. They sewed up her forehead, and bandaged her arm, and, as usual, it wasn't until it was all over that I fell apart, realizing that if the tire had been three inches the other direction it would have rolled over her head. That's when the hysteria set in. When you think about it, it's a miracle that any child survives childhood." Nadine took a sip from her water cup, then turned again to face the nurse. "Do you have brothers and sisters, Lisa?"

"I do, but I've been out of touch with most of them for awhile."

"Family problems?"

"Oh, no, nothing like that. We're just not able to travel the necessary distance to see each other. I'm hoping to get all of them together this Christmas, though."

Nadine nodded approvingly. "Families need to be together at Christmas. Mine never was, not all of us at the same time. After Danny was born, I planned to have that family portrait taken–the one I told you about–but because I was so busy with the new baby, I didn't have time to make the arrangements. The older children weren't living at home by then, so it would have taken some effort to get them all together. I just wasn't up to it, and Melvin was never one to take the initiative in anything like that."

A look of regret crossed Nadine's face. "And then it was too late. Meese was no longer with us. People kept suggesting, like you did, that I go ahead with the portrait, and have her photo superimposed, but, like I said before, it just wouldn't be the same because we wouldn't really be all together." Nadine looked pointedly at Lisa. "When your family gathers this month, you make sure you get a picture with everyone in it! I'm sure it would make your mother happy."

Lisa smiled. "Without a doubt."

"Nothing in this world is as important to a mom as seeing her children happy, and loving each other. When you have that kind of family, no amount of trouble can tear you apart."

"I can tell you love your children a great deal," stated Lisa.

"No one but another mother could ever understand how much."

"And I'm sure they love you, too."

"I have no doubt about that. But I wonder if they like me much. You see, I've always felt that, if a person loves you, it's because that person

51

is so filled with love, they can't help but scatter it around. That's why we can be commanded to love everyone. It has nothing to do with their being lovable, but only with our own capacity to love. And the development of that ability is totally incumbent upon each of us personally. But, if someone *likes* you, it's because you, yourself, have value."

"Everyone has value."

"Yes, well, maybe that's the wrong word, but I think you understand what I mean. For my children's sake, I'm glad they love me, but for myself, I just want to be liked."

"Did other people like you?"

Nadine tilted her head to one side as she considered. "They seemed to."

"Then you must have been likable."

"But other people didn't know me as well as my children did. In fact," Nadine grimaced, "I always worried that, if my friends ever found out who I really was, that would be the end of their regard."

"I don't think you were so different; no matter how well a person hides their insecurities, you can be pretty sure they still have doubts about their ability to measure up. So, how did you come up with your theory about love versus like?"

Nadine sighed. "When I was fifty, I decided to complete my degree, and one of the first classes I took was called *The Dynamics of Love*. I did a lot of soul searching that quarter, and came up with several theories, or at least ideas. One of the things I learned is that selfishness is a product of low self-esteem, rather than conceit, as we sometimes suppose. Another thing is what you just mentioned: that sometimes the biggest blowhards are those who are trying to convince themselves that they're worth something. I realized then that they deserve our understanding rather than our rejection.

"But, even though my education greatly improved my perspicacity–" Nadine laughed as Lisa's eyebrows shot up. "One of my favorite words," she explained, "but I don't get the chance to use it very often, so I have to slip it in when I can." Nadine shifted on the bed, and continued, "The trouble is, I don't know whether I actually became more tolerant, or merely became more aware that I *should* be." Her eyes flickered as she realized that she had been waxing didactic. "But you didn't come here to listen to me expound."

Lisa smiled. "I came to listen to whatever you want to tell me, or to do whatever you need me to do."

"I hope no one else discovers what a prize you are; I'd hate to have you stolen away."

"You can rest assured," Lisa declared resolutely, "that I'll be here for as long as you need me."

Early the next morning Tracey received a phone call from the care center. Miss Wills was on the line. "I hope I'm not calling at a bad time, but I just talked to the nurse who was working on the shift in question. She told me that your mother spent a peaceful night, with nothing out of the ordinary, and she doesn't remember seeing your sister here when she came off duty. I think it must have been a simple misunderstanding."

"You're probably right," Tracey conceded, although she was still baffled by her sister's totally uncharacteristic confusion. Abby just plain didn't make mistakes. "Thank you for checking, Miss Wills."

So what was up with Abigail? Had she *dreamed* the encounter with the nurse? Nadine's worsening condition had put them all under a good deal of stress, but still! Considering possible ramifications, Tracey wondered what she should do now. She couldn't see that confronting her sister with the evidence of her mistake would serve any worthwhile purpose. Was it possible that Abby could even be prematurely following in their mother's footsteps, down that thorny path to oblivion? Tracey shook her head vigorously; she wouldn't so much as entertain the notion. There had to be some other explanation. It was probably best to leave it alone, let the whole episode be forgotten. She wouldn't tell Abby that she'd already spoken with Miss Wills; she'd just ask her to put the event on the back burner, while she investigated the situation, suggesting that it would take awhile to get to the bottom of it. Hopefully, if she could stall long enough, it would all eventually blow over.

CHAPTER 4 - *Friday, December 17th*

Barry's office Christmas party was held in the dining room at Gardner Village that year. While Abigail enjoyed visiting the quaint cottages which constituted the development, offering for sale everything from oil paintings to lollipops, the party, itself, was for her more of an ordeal than a celebration. Because she only saw her husband's colleagues once a year during the holidays, she felt tongue tied and gauche in their presence. Their names were, of course, familiar, but completely detached from the corresponding faces, and she was certain that her bewilderment clearly showed. It was an enigma to her that she could call to mind countless details of business transactions, but couldn't remember faces that she hadn't seen for a few months. Fortunately, her husband didn't have that problem; she could always depend on him in sticky situations.

Abigail knew that Barry enjoyed these gatherings, so never complained about attending (at least, not in his presence), and did her best to feign a modicum of pleasure in accompanying him. He wasn't difficult to delude, since, once there, the necessary schmoozing required his full attention. Abigail managed to smile and nod, all the while wishing for a quiet corner in which to vanish.

Once dinner was served, the pressure was moderately alleviated, as their table companions were somewhat distracted by the excellent fare before them. Abigail sighed in relief, and was concentrating on her salad when she heard the inevitable question aimed in her direction, "Well, are you ready for Christmas?"

She turned to the attractive brunette at her left. "Pretty much," she replied with a smile.

"Do you have family coming?"

Abigail nodded. "My sister is actually hosting this year, but hopefully my brother and his wife will be here from Tampa, and, of course, our children and grandchildren."

"I envy you," the woman stated unexpectedly. "Both my husband and I bear the unenviable rank of 'only child,' and we, ourselves, have never been blessed with the patter of little feet."

Abigail wasn't sure what the proper response would be; she wasn't in the habit of discussing infertility problems with total strangers. "Well," she finally replied, "you never know. My mother had her last one when she was in her forties."

The woman chortled. "Thank you for the compliment, but I'm afraid I'm well past forty."

Abigail was stunned. She'd have guessed closer to thirty-five. "How do you manage to stay so young looking?"

Her companion shrugged. "Good genes."

"Hmm. Where can I get some of those?"

The woman chuckled. "My name's Cindy Spiegel, by the way. My husband was transferred here from the Chicago office, so we're relatively new in town. Consequently, I don't know any of these people."

Abigail leaned toward her, and whispered conspiratorially, "We've lived here for years, and my husband has been with the company forever, and I still don't know anyone."

A smile flickered across Cindy's lips. "Do you come to these parties often?"

"Every year, but I have no talent for remembering faces, and even less for names."

Cindy pulled her lower lip between her teeth. "Speaking of which," she drawled, "you look really familiar to me. Where did you go to school?"

"In a weather-beaten little town in Idaho that you've probably never heard of."

Cindy's eyes lit up. "Rigby, right?"

Abigail almost dropped her fork. "You know Rigby?"

"From the Ririe Highway to the Rigby Lake," she laughed. "I'm sure we must have gone to school together." Then, as she further studied Abigail's features, recognition dawned. "Lisa? Lisa Collins?"

"Close. I'm her older sister, Abigail–Abigail Bartlett. Were you a friend of hers?"

"Oh, my goodness, yes! You probably don't remember me since I was a year behind you, but I came over to your house a couple of times, and Lisa and I were in 'Annie, Get Your Gun' together when we were seniors."

"What was your maiden name?" asked Abigail.

"Winters."

Abigail explored the depths of her memory banks. "Cindy Winters." Her brow then cleared. "I do remember you! You both had the part of Annie, and played on alternating nights." Abigail leaned back in her seat and tugged on her husband's elbow. "Barry, this is an old friend of Meese's."

Barry acknowledged the introduction that followed, and marveled with Abigail over the coincidence. He made a few pertinent remarks to Cindy about her husband's position with the company, and then returned his attention to the interrupted discussion with a coworker on his other side, leaving the two women to become reacquainted.

"So, how is Lisa?" asked Cindy with a smile. "We moved away right after graduation, and I'm afraid I didn't keep in touch."

Abigail's eyes lowered. "She died several years ago."

Cindy's gasp drew the attention of various table mates, who automatically paused to ascertain the cause of her startled reaction. She smiled at each one, silently dismissing their concern, then turned back to Abigail. "I'm so sorry," she whispered.

Abigail nodded. "Thank you."

"You know, I was always a little envious of Lisa," Cindy admitted. "She was so talented; she could do anything. I don't know if you remember that Indian dance in 'Annie,' but for some reason, we ran out of rehearsal time before the choreographer had a chance to put anything together for that scene. So Lisa just went out on stage, opening night, and made it up as she went along." Cindy grunted. "I never would have had the guts to do something like that, but it didn't even phase your sister. Then, the next day, she and I got together and she helped me figure out what to do that night, when it was me in that scene."

The ensuing conversation centered around memories of Lisa, and was marked by references to warm summer evenings at the fairgrounds, winter visits to Heise Hot Springs, and the beautiful colors of autumn on Table Rock Mountain. As the hour of departure arrived,

Abigail, for the first time, regretted the winding down of the party; it had been good to reminisce about old times. As they were standing to leave, Cindy asked, "By the way, what about your mom? Is she still around?"

Abigail grimaced. "That depends on whether you're talking about her body or her mind. She's in a care center, and doesn't even know who I am anymore."

"Oh, that's hard."

"Yes, it is. For all intents and purposes, she has already left us. Only we're not allowed to mourn."

In her room at the center, Nadine sat in her wheelchair by the window, staring into the darkness outside, her mind an unfathomable mishmash of random terrors. On the other side of her door, the center was quieting down for the night. Her meds were brought in and administered, and still Nadine sat, lines of worry creasing her forehead.

Shortly after nine, her door opened and a no nonsense nurse tromped in. "Nadine, it's time for bed."

"Didn't your mother teach you how to knock?"

The nurse ignored the chastening–she was accustomed to the vagaries of senile residents–and proceeded with the task at hand. "We need to get you settled down for the night."

Nadine scowled at her. "You're not my nurse."

The woman huffed as she grabbed the handles on Nadine's wheelchair and proceeded to move her toward the bed. "Well, the center will be interested to know that, since they've been paying my salary for the last six years."

Nadine swung her arms viciously over her head, aiming at the nurse's person, and managing to land a few blows around her shoulders. The nurse quickly backed away, placing her hands on her hips. "Okay, Nadine, if that's the way you want it." She then left the room, and returned shortly with two burly attendants. With Nadine clawing and scratching, kicking and muttering, they lifted her onto the bed, then disappeared through the doorway. The nurse sighed heavily. "I'll give you a little time to cool off; then I'll come back and make sure you're okay." She left, and Nadine began to weep. Why was she in this place? When could she go home?

When the meds had had enough time to decompress Nadine's agitation, the nurse returned and pulled the covers up over her shoulders, then stood shaking her head in exasperation over the old woman's earlier tantrum. When would these people ever learn that their little tiffs bore no sway? They could abuse the staff to their heart's content, but they'd still have to spend the rest of their lives taking and following orders. Things could be a whole lot worse for them; they could be locked up in a family member's attic or basement, as in bygone years, and ignorant societies.

Attic, basement, or care center, it felt much the same to Nadine. But, in spite of her troubled mind, she slept soundly until eleven o'clock. Then, as if an alarm had been set, she lifted her head and stared at the door until it opened. A smile split her face. "Oh, I'm so glad you're finally here."

Lisa looked at her watch. "What do you mean, finally? I'm right on time."

"I wish you never had to leave. You're the only one I can talk to."

Lisa smiled as she moved around the bed, completing her nightly ritual, then settling in her usual chair. "Well, I'm here now, so what's on your mind?"

Nadine laughed. "I was just dreaming about our first farm. Jimmy, our oldest, was about six when, with some financial help from my parents, we bought two acres of land south of Salem, Utah, and built a beautiful house on it. I designed it, myself, and then we hired an independent contractor to do most of the work."

"Did you study drafting, or architecture at school?"

"No, but I used to watch my mom draw house plans. She had no training, either, just a natural ability; she designed the two houses that my parents built while I was growing up. Anyway, when the time came to do our roof, the contractor gave me a few shingling instructions, and turned me loose with hammer and nails. My mom watched the children, and I crawled around up there in the hot sun, collecting globs of tar on my pants as I went, while I single-handedly completed the job, in about two or three days, as I recall. I also stained the siding and painted the interior walls. I was in tool belt heaven, and when it was all done, I loved that house!"

"How long did it take to finish it?"

"We started it late in the spring, I believe. The contractor told us it would be completed by Thanksgiving, and I was holding him to it! Thanksgiving Day came and things weren't quite finished, but that was not going to deter us. We'd been promised to be in by Thanksgiving, and by darn, we were moving in. We had no water inside the house, only a tap out back. We didn't even have a toilet! We set up a potty chair in the back yard with a bucket underneath. There was no foliage to block the view, but the weeds were pretty tall and the neighbors were far away. It was strictly for nighttime use, though; we went to the service station if it was light out. When the contractor returned to work the day after Thanksgiving and found us living in the house, he had a small conniption, but, realizing that we were there to stay, he got a plumber on the job pronto!"

"Quite an adventure."

Nadine laughed. "One of many. I don't realize how many different things we tried until I start talking about them. Neither Melvin nor I had ever before lived on a farm, so we had a lot to learn. Someone let us board their Jersey cow in exchange for the milk, which meant that Melvin had to figure out how to coax her into giving it up."

"Did *you* ever do the milking?"

"Ha! Not me! I refused to develop that particular skill. One evening, though, after Jimmy started helping with the chores, I heard him call to me from the barn. Thinking that he might be having some kind of problem, I went running. When I got there he was calmly sitting on the stool next to the cow, with nothing seeming out of the ordinary. 'Put your hand down here a minute,' he said, indicating the cow's udder. I began to understand why I had been called, but obliged him anyway. 'Now take hold like this,' he said, and wrapped his fingers around one of the teats; I followed suit. 'Now squeeze.' I did, but deliberately failed in the attempt to produce any milk. 'See?' I said. 'I just can't do it.'"

Lisa nodded. "Smart!"

"Oh, yeah. I knew when I was well off." A touch of bitterness crept into her voice. "If I had ever learned how, it would have eventually become my responsibility, like so many other things." Nadine shook her head as if to rid it of unpleasant thoughts, and continued, "We also acquired a little maverick lamb which had to be bottle fed, and learned to come when it was called to dinner. We even had a small Welsh mare and some pigs (which I'll tell you, I grew to hate–the pigs, not the mare).

"One day, while Melvin was at work, those stupid porkers got out of their pen–or maybe they weren't so stupid. Anyway, I thought perhaps I could lasso them, so with great optimism I got a rope from the shed, and began my pursuit. I must have chased those beasts around the yard fifty times, playing jump rope all the way, before I decided that, as far as I was concerned, they could end up in someone else's stew pot. I found out later that my mom, who was living in a double wide mobile home next door, had been sitting at her window, watching the whole fracas and splitting her sides over my little exhibition."

Lisa was, by now, laughing merrily. "Did you ever get the pigs corralled again?"

"Melvin took care of it when he got home. In my own defense, though, I have to say that he wasn't able to do it alone. I think it took the whole family to finally round them up. Of course, I'm not sure whether the little kids' efforts were helping to gather or scatter. But, whichever, they were having a wonderful time."

Nadine's smile took a downward turn. "We had a little dog, got him at the pound. He was a mixed spaniel that we named Chipper, because of his happy disposition. He was a good pet, well behaved and friendly.

"The back half of our property was planted in alfalfa, and we purchased an old tractor with a mowing attachment, which we used about three times a year to harvest our crop. Melvin went out one day to begin cutting the hay, and on the way let Chipper off his chain. I climbed onto the back of the tractor, as I often did if the younger girls were napping, just to keep Melvin company while he drove. That day I begged him not to let the dog loose until he was through with his mowing. But Melvin gave no credence to my warning, so in frustration, I left the field and went back into the house to avoid witnessing what I feared would happen. Predictably, Chipper ran in front of the mower. Melvin tried to stop, but the machinery didn't respond quickly enough to avoid disaster. Both of the dog's hind legs were severed. Jimmy and Abby, who were only six and four at the time, were playing outside when the tragedy occurred, so observed the whole bloody spectacle and came screaming into the house, totally traumatized. It took me an hour to get them settled down."

"While Melvin put the dog out of his misery," declared Lisa.

Nadine looked at her in surprise. "Yes. How did you know?"

"What else could he have done? One missing leg could be compensated for, but two—" She shook her head. "Poor Chipper."

Nadine nodded and sighed. "Accidents are pretty common on a farm, but that one was just plain senseless. Well, maybe most of them are, merely a lack in good judgment. I'm thankful, though, that it was the dog and not one of the kids, although they were still having their fair share of trips to the emergency room." Nadine smiled. "It sounds as if we lived in constant peril, doesn't it?"

Lisa shrugged. "I guess it's human nature to remember the traumatic events more than the everyday incidents."

Nadine nodded. "I suppose. I often wonder what my children remember, how they perceived their parents and their home during their growing-up years. A woman once told me that, while her own memories of raising her children were filled with endless scoldings and raised voices, her kids, when they got older, only remembered the good times. I hope that's true in my case; I never had the courage to ask.

"As I recall, it was an incident which occurred on Mothers' Day a while after we moved there that began my disillusionment with that particular holiday. Until that year I had always loved the event, and wept with the other mothers over the schmaltzy stories recited from the pulpit by well-meaning men about some flawless saint of a mother (often their own), who sacrificed everything for her children. On these occasions I unfailingly felt noble and inspired, but then, all that changed.

"The one thing I never could tolerate was arriving late—anywhere!" At this admission, Lisa grinned knowingly, and Nadine continued. "That morning no one would cooperate in readying themselves for Sunday school, so we naturally reached the church after the meeting had begun.

"I was, by that point in my motherhood, accustomed to the fact that I couldn't expect to have dinner prepared for me or to be pampered in any other way, simply because it was supposed to be 'my day.' In fact, after the kids were all grown and had families of their own, Melvin invariably invited the whole gang over every Mothers' Day so that I could fix a meal for them." Nadine smirked. "Go figure. Anyway, back to that Sunday; it seemed to me that on that one day in the year my family could at least be more considerate of my feelings, and endeavor with greater zeal than usual to accommodate my whims." Nadine's tone was becoming slightly heated, and Lisa chuckled to herself.

"I fumed all through Sunday School; then afterward, as we loaded ourselves into the car so we could return home, the children commenced quibbling with each other. Well, because I had had more than enough, I simply got out, slammed the car door, and began walking. Melvin insisted on driving slowly alongside, augmenting my humiliation, while all of the children called through the open windows, offering apologies and pleading with me to join them—which I did not! Mothers' Day simply went downhill from there on." Nadine sighed. "Does your mother enjoy Mothers' Day?" she inquired of Lisa.

The young woman grimaced. "Afraid not. She's always felt undeserving of the tribute."

"Exactly!" Nadine paused, took a deep breath, and allowed her inflamed complexion to return to its normal hue.

Soon her eyes began to sparkle. "It was about that time that Abby became curious about the birds and the bees. I considered myself a very modern young mother, so gave her a rather technical explanation. Later

65

I heard her relaying my lesson to her younger sisters." She laughed. "Any similarity to what I had told her was purely coincidental."

"So, did you correct her?"

"No! It was hard enough to say it once; I couldn't bring myself to repeat it. I figured they'd eventually figure it out for themselves."

"Chicken!" Lisa laughed.

"Oh, you just wait! You'll find out how much fun it is to explain that stuff to your children."

"By the way," declared Lisa, "I met Abby the other morning when I was leaving."

"Oh? She's a good daughter," Nadine bragged.

The corners of Lisa's lips lifted slightly. "But you didn't always think so, did you." It wasn't a question.

"Why do you say that?" Nadine retorted.

"Mothers always have problems with their oldest daughters. I think they feel threatened by another female invading their territory. It's fortunate that you've been able to resolve your conflicts; at least, I assume you have. How did you manage that?"

"That's a whole other story," Nadine stifled a yawn. "I think it will have to wait for another night."

CHAPTER 5 - *Saturday, December 18th*

It was Saturday morning, the eighteenth of December, and Abigail was wrapped in her blue fleece bathrobe, sitting on the living room sofa, her dark brown hair still sleep-flattened on one side, and mascara smudges not yet washed from under her eyes. Her old photo album was spread across her knees, and she was slowly thumbing through the pages, when the front door opened, and Tracey breezed in. In one hand she was lugging a frozen bird, the handles of its mesh cover making a dent in her wrist. "They had turkeys on sale at WalMart, so I got one for the family dinner, but I don't have room in my freezer," she blurted out. "Can I put it in yours?"

Abigail looked up from her reminiscing. "Sure. Help yourself."

Tracey then noticed the open scrapbook. "What are you looking at?"

Abigail shrugged. "Just taking a stroll down memory lane. Care to join me?"

"First let me get rid of my fat friend here." She made her way through the kitchen, and stepped into the garage, where she hefted her burden into the old Amana. She then returned to the welcome warmth of the living room. "Why the sudden yen for yesteryear? It's been ages since you looked at those old photos."

"I ran into someone last night who knew Meese in high school. It got me thinking about when we were kids. Come sit for awhile; you're not in a hurry, are you?"

Tracey lifted a shoulder. "I guess I can stay for a minute." She dropped her coat over the back of a chair and flounced down beside her sister, crowding in close and taking half of the album onto her lap.

"All these pictures have reminded me about the family portrait that Mom wanted so much," Abigail lamented. "I feel bad that she never got it. I should have made it happen. I was old enough to show a little initiative. What was I so busy doing that I couldn't take the time?"

"I'm not sure we knew it was that important to her."

"What do you mean? It's all she talked about that Christmas. As soon as she got Danny home from the hospital, she wanted a family portrait taken. She kept telling us that she was going to make an appointment with the photographer. And I just waited for her to do it, instead of offering to step in. I know now what I didn't then, that she was just too busy with Danny. I didn't realize until I had babies of my own how time consuming they can be. And he was especially so with all of his health problems."

"How could we have done it, anyway, with him being so sick?" Tracey countered.

"A photographer could have come to the house. It wasn't impossible, just inconsequential, I guess, to everyone except Mom. And then, I always expected that she could take care of everything that needed doing. I don't think I really understood what a difficult time that was for her, with Danny."

"Don't beat yourself up, Sis. You weren't the only one who let her down. As I recall, we were all pretty wrapped up in ourselves at that time. Jimmy had just got a job and moved out; you were in school, just home for the holidays; and even though I was living there, I was pregnant with Alan, and feeling pretty sorry for myself."

Abigail turned her eyes soulfully toward her sister. "That's right. You had a few concerns of your own right then, didn't you."

A smile flickered across Tracey's lips. "The bottom line is, we all tend to get involved with battling through our own agendas and sometimes forget that we're not the only one who is struggling. Others are not always able to meet our needs, but I think they, and we, for the most part do the best we can. There was a lot going on, with all of us, right after Danny was born."

Abigail shook her head. "In some ways, that all seems like another life, but at the same time, it feels like yesterday." Her brow furrowed as she threw an arm around her sister's shoulders. "How did we get so old, Trace?"

They laughed together, the sound peeling away the years, then Abigail turned a page of the album, and they simultaneously gasped as the face of their deceased sister looked up at them.

"I wish Meese were still here," Abigail sighed mournfully.

"Do you think we'll ever get over the hurt?" asked Tracey as tears began to pool in her lower lids. "We were the Three Musketeers; I still feel like a third of me is missing."

"People tell you it gets easier, and I guess it does, but it never gets easy. I still miss her like my right arm." Abigail ran a finger across her moist cheek. "You know that nurse I told you about? The one who claimed to talk to Mom?"

Tracey huffed. "Abby, I thought we agreed . . ."

"No," Abigail interrupted, "I'm not–" She lifted her hand in a motion of negation. "It's just that she looked a lot like Meese. Kinda shocked me when I first saw her."

"You didn't tell me about that."

"I guess I was so stunned by what she said that I kind of forgot about how she looked. The idea that Mom might have actually spoken to her intelligibly more or less wiped everything else from my mind. Anyway, there's a remarkable resemblance. Oh, and by the way, her name's Lisa."

"You're kidding! How weird is that?"

"I know," Abigail concurred. "And it was strange, because it didn't make me sad, coming face to face with our sister's twin. She seemed really pleasant and sweet, just like our Meese, and I felt reasonably comfortable around her." She pursed her lips, waiting for Tracey's response, but her younger sibling, for once, was rendered speechless.

"Oh, by the way," Abigail went on, "Barry and I are driving Dad over to see Mom this evening and I wondered if you and Dale would like to meet us there and then go to dinner at Applebee's."

Tracey was agreeable and they set the time for five o'clock. Abigail would prefer to always have her sister in attendance when she called on Nadine, but unfortunately, the constraints on Abigail's time, for the most part, prohibited joint visits. As chagrined as it made her feel, the truth was that their mother was always in a better mood when Tracey was present; she occasionally even recognized her. Maybe it was because Tracey had never really grown up; despite her many scrapes along the sharp edges of life's vicissitudes, she had maintained the vibrancy and enthusiasm—not to mention the occasional ponytail—of her youth.

If Abigail didn't love her sister so much, it would have been easy to hate her. Somehow able to disregard the emotional wounds of her past, Tracey continued to act the eternal teen-ager, bouncing through life on a pogo stick of optimism. Abigail often wondered how she could maintain her youthful, radiant persona, while carrying heartaches that might easily have destroyed anyone else.

Tracey and Dale were ten minutes late in arriving at the center and Abigail was relieved that it wasn't the usual twenty or thirty. Tracey hugged her father, exchanged the usual greetings, and then turned to Abigail. "Have you heard from Jimmy?" she inquired. "Are they still planning to be here for Christmas?"

Her sister nodded. "They're coming on the twenty-third. Since you're doing the family dinner this year, I've invited them to stay at my place." Both sisters were excited about their brother's expected arrival. It had been two years since he and his wife had last paid a visit. At one time, he may have been the pesky, annoying big brother, but years and maturity have a way of whitewashing past indiscretions. He was now their hero.

They found Nadine in her room, scrunched down in her wheelchair with her head lolled forward, either sleeping or pretending. "Hey, Mom," intoned Tracey. "The gang's all here."

Nadine's eyes slowly opened as she lifted her head, her brow creasing in concentration. "Who is it?"

"It's Tracey, Mom, and Abby and Dad. Barry and Dale are here, too."

But Nadine was not interested in who might be coming to call. "Tracey, I'm so worried."

"Why, Mom?"

Nadine grasped her daughter's hand. "You need to be careful. You can't trust them!"

"Who? Who can't I trust?"

Nadine's terror filled eyes switched from side to side, as if to check out a possible security breach. "I have to warn you. You've got to do something. You just don't know!"

"I'm fine, Mom. You need to stop worrying."

"No! You don't understand!" Her whole body swung from side to side as she shook her head in despair. "Oh, you just don't understand!"

"Mom, I'm okay. We're all okay." Tracey made a wide gesture with her arm to indicate the others in the room.

Nadine's eyes slowly panned the area, then studied each of the strangers who surrounded her chair. Finally they came to rest on her husband. "Do I know you?"

Melvin grunted. He leaned forward and took her hand, which she immediately withdrew. "You've known me for more than sixty years, Sweetheart. I'm your husband."

Nadine curled her lip. "In your dreams, Frog-face!" She then switched her attention to Abigail. "Lucile, tell these people to leave," she ordered, reaching toward her elder daughter. "I have to talk to you."

"Lucile's your sister, Mom. I'm Abby, your daughter."

Nadine jerked her hand back. "You're too old to be Abby. You're just here to get my money. Get out! All of you!"

"Mom," Abigail pleaded.

"No! No! No!" She raised her hands to defend herself. "Go away before I call the police!"

Abigail shrugged at her sister and left the room, followed by Barry, with Melvin on his arm. "I hate seeing your mother like this," Melvin lamented, pulling a handkerchief from his back pocket and loudly blowing his nose.

Abigail mentally cringed at the all too familiar sound. Her father had never been especially couth when it came to performing that particular ritual and had often grossed her out in the middle of a church meeting, during basketball games (when one could have sworn that the time

72

keeper's horn had beeped), and even while the family was enjoying ('til then) their evening meal. No one at the rest home seemed to notice, however. They were undoubtedly accustomed to that sort of thing . . . or worse.

"I'm sorry, Dad," she apologized for her mother's offensive behavior. "Maybe you shouldn't come any more. She won't know whether you do or don't."

Melvin shook his head sorrowfully. "I don't know. I don't know."

Abigail laid her arm across her father's shoulders, offering solace. "It's hard on all of us, Dad. I just feel like she isn't even my mom any more."

Melvin's stooped body stiffened. "She'll always be your mom. Don't you ever forget that."

Abigail sighed in frustration. Well, she'd bombed out again. She never had possessed the ability to say just the right thing. Not like Tracey of the silver tongue. Tracey, who had never met a man—or woman—she couldn't charm. Tracey, who seemed to have the world by the tail. Tracey, whom Abigail admired, envied, scolded, and adored.

Abigail was suddenly reminded, yet again, of her conversation with the night nurse Lisa. Thus far she had abided by Tracey's wishes to let her handle it, but something about the way Nadine had just dismissed them frustrated her to the point that she was determined to get to the bottom of whatever was going on. And if her sister wasn't going to actively pursue it, she'd do it, herself. She looked toward her mother's door just as Tracey and Dale emerged. "I know I agreed not to bug you about this, but did you ever find out anything about what that nurse told me?" she asked her sister.

Tracey's shoulders drooped. She had hoped to avoid any discussion of the subject. "I talked to Miss Wills, the administrator. Now *there's* a piece of work! She made me feel like I was back in third grade." Tracey straightened her spine, puckered her lips, and launched into an exaggerated impersonation. "'Well, my dear, since you couldn't possibly know anything about anything, it would, in my opinion, be futile to investigate the circumstances, but if you insist, I'll see what I can do.'" Tracey rolled her eyes.

Abigail giggled in spite of herself. "And did she?"

Tracey huffed uncomfortably. "She said that she checked, but couldn't find anyone who'd spoken with you."

"And you didn't bother to tell me that?"

"I didn't want you to get upset, like you're starting to do right now."

"I'm not getting upset."

"Are too."

"Am not!"

"Are too. Look, I think we just need to forget it. No one really seems to know what happened."

Abigail gave her a dubious look. "So, what are you saying? You think I'm as nuts as Mom?" Then, realizing how her words may have offended, she turned to her father. "Sorry, Dad; I didn't mean that." Melvin nodded his head, his eyes sorrowful, and Abigail continued. "I know what I saw and heard, Tracey; I didn't dream the whole thing."

"Well, actually," Tracey muttered, "I wonder if that's exactly what you did do."

Abigail stopped in her tracks and stared at her sister. "You *do* think I'm nuts." Her eyes began to fill, which, in turn, triggered her anger. "Have I ever given you reason to think I've lost it?"

"No," soothed Tracey, "of course not. But we're all under a lot of stress with Mom the way she is. It's not unreasonable that you'd dream about her. And some dreams are so vivid, they do seem like they're real. I've had a few like that, myself. I'm just saying, it's possible."

"Tracey, you of all people should know that I don't confuse reality with fantasy. How could you insinuate such a thing?" She stared incredulously at her sister. "I'm suddenly not hungry. Why don't you all go on without me? Barry can drop me off at home."

"C'mon, Abby. I only meant that no one thinks what you described is even possible. People like Mom don't suddenly snap out of it."

"I'm not suggesting that she's cured. Obviously. I'm just saying that maybe she had a few moments of sanity." Abigail dug into her purse for a tissue, and held it to her eyes. "I wanted it to be true."

Tracey moved toward her sister and put her arms around her. "Abby, no one wants that more than I do. I'm sure there's a logical explanation, and I promise we'll get to the bottom of it. But, for tonight, let's just forget it and go have dinner." She gave her sister the pleading look that usually got her what she wanted. "Deal?"

Abigail blew her nose and hiccuped, which made them both giggle. When their eyes met, they were done for; pent up emotions exploded into gales of laughter, though neither of them knew exactly what was so funny. Finally, Abigail took a deep breath. "Okay," she relented. "But promise me you'll find that nurse."

Tracey lifted her hand, and with a haughty look, dramatically crossed her heart, bringing on more laughter. She then linked arms with her sister and coaxed her along, finally forcing her into a fair impersonation of Dorothy and her fanciful companions, as the two women, in childlike abandon, executed the Yellow Brick Road hop-skip to their parked cars.

Even though Abigail had vowed to forget the episode with Lisa, it continued to prey upon her mind, putting a damper on her spirits for the rest of the evening. And, though she had firmly reprimanded Tracey

75

for suggesting that she may have momentarily blurred the line between reality and illusion, she silently wondered to herself if she had done just that. Worst case scenario: was this the beginning of her own descent into that province of nonexistence which plagued her mother?

CHAPTER 6 - *Sunday, December 19ᵗʰ*

Abigail couldn't shake the blues all the next day. She wanted so much to have her mother back, if only for a moment. Why should the nurse be permitted to glimpse her one episode of sanity (if, indeed, she had), while her own daughters were denied that blessing? Abigail needed time with her mom to ask for forgiveness, and offer her own, for all of the offenses of a lifetime. She'd never imagined that her chances would run out.

She remembered how her mom had hated Mothers' Day, and now, after struggling through a few of her own, she understood why. One particular Sunday came to mind, when Abigail had attended church and listened as a man told the story of his "angel" great-grandmother. According to his tale, the woman was at home one morning, alone with her children. Her husband was on a cattle drive, or some such, and wouldn't be back for several days. She had gone outside to the woodpile to bring in some kindling for the kitchen stove, and a rattle snake, hiding among the split logs, struck her on the arm as she lifted her load.

Casting aside all concern for her own well being, she cooked and baked, laundered and cleaned, so that, following her imminent death, her children's needs would be seen to until their father returned. Miracle of miracles! Because of her increased activity, the poison was purged from her system, and she lived!

Abigail snorted to herself. "I always thought excessive exertion just pushed the venom through your body faster, and brought death on sooner." Well, true or not, it was that kind of story that put a blight on motherhood. Who could possibly measure up? Thank goodness, at today's meeting, she at least wouldn't be exposed to the maudlin ruminations of someone's delusional grandson.

Normally, the Sunday before Christmas was Abigail's favorite Sabbath; she had forever loved the music and sentiment of the season. The church services included carols by the choir and sermons about the Savior: his birth and life. As Abigail listened to the presentations, she considered the miracles that Jesus had performed while on the earth, but rather than experiencing the sweetness that usually accompanied her reverent reflections, she bitterly wondered, "Why not me? Why not my mom?"

Their dinner that evening was a somber affair, the only conversation being, "Please pass the salt and pepper," and, "Did you get the snow blower running?"

At Tracey's house, carols were pumped out through the iPod speakers, football players romped across the television screen, and grandchildren encircled the diningroom table, boisterously involved in a game of Uno Attack. Tracey and her daughter were holed up in the bedroom, seeking a tranquil spot for quiet conversation.

"So how are you feeling?" asked the concerned mom.

"Just like I always feel when I'm two months pregnant," replied Jaimee with a grimace. "Sometimes I wonder why I keep putting myself through this: nine months of misery, culminating in eight hours of torture."

Tracey chuckled. She knew it was her daughter's present discomfort doing the talking. "But the rewards are so sweet," she reminded her.

"Yeah. My friend says that babies are like potato chips; you're never satisfied with just one."

"Amazing, isn't it, how our love stretches enough to surround all of our children? And how it never diminishes? I remember Mom saying that she sometimes got really tired of being a mother, but couldn't find a way to resign. I guess some mothers could, and do. But Mom was incapable of denying her love for us."

"Is Grandma doing any better?"

Tracey shook her head. "I'm sure it's just a matter of time."

"Poor Grandma," Jaimee sympathized. "Doesn't seem fair."

Tracey reached up a hand to smooth her daughter's hair. "Since when is 'fair' a part of life? I guess it all contributes to our earthly education, though I'm not sure, right now, what Grandma's situation is teaching us. Patience, maybe. I admit I could use a few pointers on that subject." She lifted her eyebrows. "I guess someday we'll understand. I'll tell you this much: if I ever get to the point where Grandma is, just dig a hole and throw me in, education be darned."

"I wish I could go see her more often, but with my schedule, it's almost impossible."

Tracey patted her daughter's arm. "Like I told your Aunt Abby, not too long ago, we do the best we can. Grandma doesn't really know if you're there or not anyway."

At the care center, Nadine passed the evening seated in the front hallway, sullenly staring through the large windows into the well-lit atrium. She watched as the wind wrestled with crystalized tree branches, swirling their load of fluff across the frozen ground, the wintry scene indicative of the rime that imprisoned her own thoughts. Even the joyful music of carolers, who roamed the halls offering their particular brand of cheer, failed to penetrate her gloom. Greetings from staff members were met with withering looks, snide remarks, and ugly epithets.

At nine o'clock a CNA pushed her to her room and helped settle her for the night. The nurse came in and administered her meds, which she accepted without incident, and finally she was left alone. She then slept until the expected opening of the door awakened her. With a happy sigh she waved a knobby hand. "Is it snowing out?" she asked.

"It is," Lisa acknowledged, "but it's falling sideways. Reminds me of Idaho."

"You lived in Idaho?" Nadine was intrigued. "I did, too. So I know what you mean by oblique snowfall. I used to get so depressed when the wind would blow–which, in Idaho, was all of the time!"

Lisa smiled her concurrence as she seated herself beside the bed. "The other night I believe you were going to tell me about Abigail, and how your relationship changed."

"Hmm, you have a good memory." Nadine paused, deliberating. "We'll get to that, but first I want to tell you about our move to Idaho. Melvin's company transferred him to Idaho Falls when Tracey was about three. The farther away my beloved Utah mountains receded, the harder I bawled. I don't think I dried my tears for four months."

"Why was that such a hard thing for you?"

"I loved Utah. I had family there, and long term friends. The town we lived in, Salem, was rural and we were acquainted with everyone. When we first moved there, the people were so cordial, they welcomed us with open arms. I was content to spend the rest of our lives there and had thought, when we built that house, that that's exactly what we'd do. But Melvin didn't dare turn down this new job offer. It meant a more prestigious position with the company, as well as a major increase in salary. Also, if he'd declined, that would have been the end of his progress, as far as his career was concerned. So, we had little choice but to load up and go.

"We luckily found a home right away; it was on three acres just north of town. We bought a cow and a couple of green colts, and then asked every cowboy in the area for information about breaking horses. Each one offered a different set of instructions, so we simply threw caution to the wind, saddles on their backs, and good sense to the four corners. We managed to get thrown a few times, but we eventually learned, and so did our faithful steeds."

"Did you ever get hurt?" Lisa asked.

"Oh, our horses weren't the bucking broncos you see on television. When we got thrown it was more like slipping to the ground, and was due to our own lack of experience rather than any violent behavior on the animal's part. My biggest fear was getting a foot caught in the stirrup and being dragged. We used to see a lot of that in the movies, and I had nightmares about what it would do to me. My mare was a bit more skittish than Melvin's, so I spent more time climbing back on than he did, but once I got her broke, she was like riding a rocking chair.

"We loved our animals, and once again were in the market for a dog. I watched the paper and, one day, noticed an ad for a six-month old German shepherd at a greatly reduced price. He was the last of the litter and had been kept outside, away from human contact, for most of his six months. After bringing him home, I put him in the garage while I fed the family and put the children to bed. Melvin was working late that night, so I was alone with the dog and used the time to get acquainted.

From that night on he was exclusively my own pet. He tolerated Melvin and the children, but I was the one he tagged after and slept next to."

"You let a German shepherd sleep with you?" Lisa guffawed.

"Not quite," chuckled Nadine. "He slept on the floor next to my side of the bed. He was so smart, it only took me three days to completely housebreak him, so he lived inside with us and was my protector, big time. I remember once when our septic system got backed up and I was beside myself, worrying over how we'd ever get it repaired (there was never any money, and it was just before the holidays).

"A friend of mine came over one day to visit and I was explaining to her our stinky dilemma, and because I was so overwrought I began to cry. Well, Dan, the dog, thought my friend was causing my tears and immediately went into attack mode, baring his teeth and growling. He always obeyed me, though, without question, so all I had to do was tell him it was okay.

"Actually, my friend had just come over to ask if I would be interested in working with her in the spud harvest to make some extra money for Christmas. Naturally, I agreed, and we were subsequently hired by one of the local farmers. As it turned out, however, her husband refused to allow her to perform such exhausting, dirty labor, so I was left on my own.

"As I rode the combine, the fine dust stirred up by the motion of the equipment filled my nose, mouth, ears, and even my eyes with dark soil so that, in spite of my nightly scrubbing, I awoke each morning with swollen eyes, and muddy tears running down my cheeks. I only lasted three days, earning about fifty dollars, but I certainly gained an added appreciation for my children, who later did it every year for the full two weeks of harvest.

"But, getting back to Dan; because he was so devoted to me, it was several weeks before he would even go outside by himself to take a potty break. I mean, he was right at my side, twenty-four, seven. Then, one morning just a few months after we got him, he uncharacteristically followed the children through the front door when they went out to catch the school bus. I assumed he would relieve himself and come right back, so I wasn't concerned. A few seconds later I heard a yelp, and fearing the worst, went running out to see what had happened. There was Dan, lying on the road behind the back tire of the bus; the driver hadn't even seen him.

"I rushed onto the road, hoping to find him still alive, but his body merely twitched a couple of times, and then lay still. I burst into tears, and screamed to Melvin, who was still in the house. He came out, picked Dan up, and carried him to the back yard where we buried him. I'd never owned such a sweet, allegiant pet, and it broke my heart. I cried all day, every day, for a week and swore I'd never own another dog."

"You had some pretty tough luck with dogs, didn't you?"

"Well, as it turned out, this particular loss was a blessing in disguise. In spite of my former determination to remain pet free, after a while I started looking for another shepherd and again saw an ad in the paper. I phoned, but there was no answer. For three days I kept trying to get hold of the owners, but could never contact them. I was sure, by that time, that the dog was long gone to someone else, but I kept hoping. Finally, when I dialed the number one last time, the other end was picked up, but no one said anything for a few seconds. Then there was a tentative, 'Hello.'

"I explained to the woman the reason for my call and she informed me that the dog was still available. 'I just found out,' she said, 'that our telephone has been out of order for the last three days, so even though we could call out, no one could call in. I was just picking it up to report the problem to the repair service. I guess you had just dialed my number and were already on the line.'"

"Pretty bizarre," commented Lisa.

"Oh, that's only the beginning of the story. Unlike Dan, this new dog Adolph–so named by his former owners–loved my children and made them his number one priority. He had only been with us about two weeks when Tracey fell into the irrigation ditch that ran along the other side of the road in front of our house. Adolph, always near, jumped into the ditch after her, forced himself beneath her body and pushed her up until her head was above the edge of the bank. He then kept her there until a neighbor boy noticed and completed the rescue. So," Nadine reflected, "if Dan hadn't died, and if that woman's phone hadn't been out of order, Tracey would most certainly have drowned that day."

"A miracle," remarked Lisa.

"Definitely a miracle," concurred Nadine. "All the little details had to work in concert for things to happen the way they did for Tracey to be saved. I have a friend who used to say, 'Coincidence is when God chooses to remain anonymous.' I like that. Speaking of miracles brings to mind the night, a few years later, when Melvin and I were in the car, headed into town. It was pitch black and foggy, and we had to cross two sets of railroad tracks on the way, only one of which had a warning light, so we were going slowly.

"All of a sudden, right in front of us was the blinking red crossing light. Melvin slammed on the brakes just as a train whooshed past. It couldn't have missed us by more than a few inches. The whole car shook. When it was gone, we looked at each other and took a deep breath, both of us scared out of our wits. Then we noticed that the light we had seen was no longer in front of us. We were actually at the other tracks, the ones with no warning signal. The red light which had seemed to each of us to be no more than a couple of feet away was actually two miles down the road at the highway intersection."

"I guess it wasn't your time to go yet," observed Lisa.

"Well, we did have some children to raise. And that was a full time job, with never a dull moment, a job that also encompassed a few other miracles. When Jimmy was about seven or eight, Melvin was in the unfortunate habit of siphoning gasoline from the car to use in the lawn mower, probably because he didn't have the money to buy more gas. Of course, our children were always attentive to the things they'd have been better off not witnessing. So, one evening, Jimmy decided to follow his father's example. I had just put dinner on the table and was calling everyone to come and eat.

"The door to the garage opened and in staggered Jimmy, reeking of gasoline. I knew immediately what had happened, but didn't know what to do about it, so stood there bolted to the floor as his eyes began to roll back into his head. Suddenly, it was like an unseen something took control of my body. I walked to the table, grabbed a glass of milk, and held it to Jimmy's lips. He never questioned my reasons, but gulped it down obediently. It was years before I learned that milk is the proper antidote for gasoline poisoning."

"So he was all right?" asked Lisa.

"He was fine. He climbed up to the table and we had dinner! Again, after it was over, I agonized about what might have happened if Someone hadn't been watching over us.

"After living in our Idaho Falls house for a few years we decided to do the farming thing on a grand scale and eventually traded our home for forty-five acres in Rigby. There was no dwelling on the property and we couldn't afford to build, so we advertised in the paper for a house to be moved.

"I won't bore you with all of the intricacies of that adventure, only to say that we found a wonderful old house on a lot across the street from the hospital in Idaho Falls. All of the dwellings on that block had to be removed to make room for a new medical building. At the very first look I knew that old place was destined to become our future residence. I obtained the key from the hospital administrator, and after touring the inside of the house, refused to give it back. They'd call and say, 'We have someone who would like to see that house, and we need the key.' But I'd just put them off, telling them we were going to buy it; I just needed time to find a mover. I'm sure they were becoming very annoyed with me, but they never got their key back, anyway.

"I had to call companies all over the west coast before I finally found someone who would take on the formidable challenge of moving such a monstrously huge structure. Then, on the scheduled day of transport, knowing that the snail-paced procession would be unbearable to watch, I impatiently waited at home and attempted to estimate their travel time so that I would arrive at the farm concurrently with the delivery.

"I had, however, optimistically miscalculated, so it was necessary to do a bit of backtracking until I finally found them about a mile away. They were just getting ready to cross a wooden bridge that had obviously seen better days. I pulled into a nearby field and climbed out of my car to watch–apprehensively I might add–as the driver of the tow truck cautiously rolled his front wheels onto the old timbers. There was a good deal of creaking and groaning, but everything seemed okay until the house, itself, started across. Then there was this terrible sound of fracturing wood and I knew that disaster was imminent. I stood there and helplessly watched as my beloved house tilted and plunged into the irrigation canal. It felt like my heart dropped at the same velocity and landed in the pit of my stomach with equal force. All of my relentless work had come to naught; we still didn't have a home.

"I ran to the moving truck and cried to the driver, "What are we going to do now?"

"He alighted from the cab and walked to the edge of the canal. 'We'll have to get some equipment in here to jack the house up and get it back onto the trailer,' he informed me. Then, noticing my aggrieved countenance, he added, 'Don't worry. You'll still have your house.'

"It took them a week to lift it out of the ditch, but fortunately little damage was done. They built houses to endure anything in those days, even an unprecedented drop in the drink."

Lisa giggled. "Where did that expression come from?"

"Drop in the drink? It was one my daddy used to use. I heard it so much, I guess I never realized that everyone doesn't understand what it means. Tracey used to always laugh at my use of idioms; most of them were handed down from my parents."

Nadine chuckled. "I told my kids a story once, about a woman who always cut the ends off her ham before placing it into the oven to bake. One day her daughter asked her why she did that. 'I don't know,' she said. 'It's just what my mom always did. Why don't you ask her?' So the little girl goes to her grandma and asks, 'Grandma, how come you always cut the ends off of your ham before you bake it?' 'I don't know,' says the grandma. 'It's just what my mother always did. Why don't you ask her?' So the little girl asks her great-grandma, 'Why do you always cut off the ends of your ham before you bake it?' 'Well,' says Great-grandma, 'that's all the bigger my pan is.'"

Lisa enjoyed the anecdote, and Nadine appreciated her merriment. "After I told that story, whenever I used a phrase that Tracey hadn't heard before, she'd say, 'Pig in a pan, Mom. Pig in a pan.' And then it got so, no matter how common a saying was, if it was even slightly idiomatic, she'd always come back with her 'pig in a pan.'

"Anyway, once our house was delivered, I drove to Rigby every day and did repairs, anxiously awaiting the time when we could take occupancy. The only major renovation we did was to create a larger kitchen by combining a room and a half. We turned the other half into a walk-in closet off the master bedroom. Other than that, it was mostly painting and paneling. Soon after we moved in, however, we discovered that the walls and ceiling contained no insulation whatsoever. It was November in Idaho and it was cold! The kids all wore their winter coats in the house and I stayed wrapped up in a blanket, doing nothing all day but working on a jigsaw puzzle, which I had purchased just for that purpose.

"We hired a company to take care of the problem, but before they came, Melvin had to bore holes through the inside walls of the house, between each pair of studs, so the insulation material could be blown in. Well, when he drilled one of the holes in the newly formed closet, he didn't bother to check the other side of the wall and didn't realize that there was already an opening on the bathroom side." Nadine's expression clearly indicated her annoyance with Melvin's long-ago lack of heed. "On about the third day of the project, one of the workmen called out, 'Mrs. Collins, would you mind coming here a minute?' I drew my quilt around me and followed his voice into the bathroom. 'There's a small problem here,' he explained. 'I was blowing insulation into this hole for half an hour and it just wouldn't fill up, and well, you'd better look for yourself.' I opened the door between the bathroom and the walk-in closet and sloshed into the missing insulation–waist deep.

Needless to say, I was picking powdered yuck out of my clothes for months!

"Meanwhile, a problem with the living room fireplace had to be addressed. The original bricks had become dangerously loosened during our home's transportation–and, of course, its swim in the canal–so the plan was to remove them completely and insert a more efficient metal lining into the recess. Jimmy, then a strapping young man of fifteen, came into the room as I was meticulously pulling out one brick at a time and stacking them behind me on the floor. He watched for a few minutes and then said, 'At that rate you'll never get the job done.'

"He left the room, and the next thing I knew, there he was with the sledge hammer in hand. He told me I'd better stand back, and I willingly removed myself to the opposite corner of the room, where I watched, mesmerized, as he wielded his tool of destruction. At his first blow an avalanche of bricks and soot plummeted through the floor and into the basement. Jimmy vaulted backward to avoid a premature burial, and there the two of us stood in wide-eyed wonder. When the dust began to clear, we hesitantly made our way toward the edge of the newly created cavity in the flooring and gazed downward. There was a sizeable heap of debris in the middle of the basement, where a child's bedroom had been planned, and I said to Jimmy, 'It looks like one of the girls is already living there.'

"'Dad's going to have a fit,' was Jimmy's only concern." Nadine gave Lisa a chagrined look. "Melvin, it's true, was not thrilled. He shook his head and sighed a lot." Nadine then lowered her voice to simulate Melvin's baritone. "'The only way we can get the mess out of there is to load the bricks into buckets and hand them out the basement window to the kids, so they can dump them outside. And then we'll have to get someone in here to rebuild the living room floor.'" Nadine rolled her eyes. "Okay, so let's get at it."

Lisa's enjoyment of the yarn was evidenced by her prolonged giggling, and even Nadine had to chuckle, although she hadn't considered it totally amusing at the time. "By and by, it all got taken care of; the floor was mended, the chimney replaced, and the fireplace installed." She heaved a sigh. "Ah, the stuff memories are made of."

Lisa grinned and nodded, then glanced toward the window. "It looks like the wind has stopped." She stood and crossed the room, cupped her hands around her eyes and pressed them against the glass, peering out. "It's still snowing, though."

"You know, as much as I hated those Idaho winters, there's nothing I'd like better, right now, than to go outside and watch the flakes fall."

Lisa gave her a conspiratorial look. "I'm up to it, if you are."

Nadine grunted softly. "Isn't that against the rules?"

"I'll be with you all the time. You'll be safe."

"But won't you get into trouble?"

"Only if someone finds out."

Nadine's eyes fairly danced. "A nefarious adventure! Let's do it!"

Lisa assisted Nadine into the wheelchair, pulled the blankets from the bed and gathered a couple of extra ones from the closet to wrap around the old woman. When she was thoroughly bundled, the two of them made their way to the door. Lisa pulled it open, stuck her head out, and then turned back to Nadine. "Looks like the coast is clear." She grabbed the handles of the chair and speedily steered it toward the outside exit, entered the proper code, and maneuvered Nadine through the opening.

"I don't believe I've tried sneaking around since I was five," exclaimed Nadine in a tone which indicated clearly that she thought she may have been missing out.

"You want to just sit here," asked Lisa, "or would you rather I push you for awhile?"

"Oh," Nadine sighed, "let's walk. Could we possibly go around the block?"

"We can give it a try."

Conscientious home owners had cleared the sidewalks earlier in the evening and what snow had amassed since then was soft and pristine, but still amounted to a few inches on top of the concrete. However, at some point in their hurried departure from the center Lisa had managed to don a pair of heavy boots, evidently with good traction. And her slight build apparently belied the fact of her strength, for the accumulated white stuff proved to be of little hindrance as she pushed Nadine along their chosen route.

Turning the corner they beheld the glowing confetti of Christmas lights, which hung from every house, tree, and bush on either side of the street, their reflection bouncing merrily from Nadine's eyes. "Talk about 'the luster of mid-day,'" she remarked. Then, leaning her head back, she gazed upward, noticing how the flakes seemed to form and fall from just a few feet above. The awesome sight stirred up within her memories from the past. "The first time I ever saw snow, my daddy explained to me how each flake is different; of all of the billions that fall, no two are alike. One of the many examples of infinite creation which I couldn't then, nor do I now, fathom. We live in an amazing world, full of beauty; we should be grateful every day of our lives."

"And have you been?" Lisa was asking out of pure interest, not as any kind of reprimand.

91

"No," Nadine admitted. "Like everyone else, I've done my share of grumbling, mostly over inconsequential things. It took me a long time to learn how to 'be still, and know that [He] is God.' The lowly elements are often smarter than we humans; they've always known how to be still, like they are right now. Isn't it quiet when everything is snuggled up under a blanket of snow?

"It reminds me of one Christmas when I decided that I wanted to cut our own tree. It was shortly after Abby was married. She and Barry and Danny and I drove to a forest in Idaho–I can't remember exactly where it was, but I know we had to stop at the ranger station on the way and get a permit to cut. Melvin was working, so couldn't go with us, and Danny was just little, so poor Barry was the only man along and had to do all the work.

"But I remember how quiet it was. There was no one but the four of us in sight, and none of us talked much at first; I think we didn't want to break the spell. As I recall, there wasn't a lot of snow on the ground, maybe a couple of feet. It was crusted so hard we could walk on top of it for the most part, and I remember the crunching sound our boots made. Once in a while someone would hit a soft spot and fall through to their knees, which would throw them off balance so they toppled over. And, of course, if anyone else was close by, the one who fell would purposely pull the other person down with him. That always started us laughing and carrying on, until all of us were down on the ground, rubbing each others' faces in the snow.

"Somehow, we didn't feel the cold, though. I think we were warmed from the inside out that day, just being together with people we loved."

"Did you find the tree you wanted?" asked Lisa.

"Oh, yes. We had to choose from among the ones that had been tagged earlier by the forest service, so, of course, our options were limited. I think we just kept trudging around, searching for the perfect specimen, until every one of us was so worn out that all of the trees began to look good. So we just picked one. But all through that season, whenever I looked at our tree, I was filled with the same feelings I'd had on the day we cut it—well, on the day Barry cut it: warm and happy."

They continued their walk in silence, Nadine drawing in deep breaths, reveling in the unique fragrance of a snowy night, while Lisa found pleasure in affording her the luxury. Finally, they reluctantly approached the side entrance to the care center. "How can I thank you, Lisa?" The tears in Nadine's eyes did not spring up entirely as an effect of the cold weather. "At your age you still have many 'firsts' to look forward to. When you're as old as I, there are only 'lasts.' This is the last time I'll ever see the houses decorated with Christmas lights, or be out amidst a gentle snowfall. Thank you."

Lisa bent and placed a kiss on Nadine's forehead. "You're welcome. But I think you may still have one or two 'firsts' left. You just never know." She opened the door, checked the nurses' station and the hallways, and hastily wheeled Nadine to her room, where she settled her, once again, into bed.

"It's getting late," Lisa smiled, "or maybe I should say 'early.' You'd better get some sleep. I'll be back tomorrow night, so think of some good stuff to tell me."

"Are you sure you want to hear more?" Nadine was skeptical, but hopeful. What else brought an old woman such pleasure as reliving her memories?

"I want to hear everything," Lisa assured her. "But we don't have to do it all at once. There's still time." She pushed the button to lower Nadine's head, then pulled up the covers and favored the old woman with another kiss on her forehead. "Would it help you fall asleep if I sang to you?" she offered.

"I'd love that," Nadine said. "Meese's favorite was 'When Someone Cares.' You probably don't know that one, though; it's an oldie."

"As a matter of fact, I do," Lisa acknowledged. "I remember my mother singing it." In a soft soprano she began, and as the message of the song wrapped itself around Nadine's heart, she could almost imagine that her beloved daughter was at her bedside.

CHAPTER 7 - *Monday, December 20th*

As the first suggestion of daylight filtered through the bedroom window on Monday morning, Tracey fought against her unavoidable ascent into consciousness. The vestiges of a night vision were clinging relentlessly to the edges of her mind, images that she wanted desperately to retain. She hadn't dreamed about Meese for a couple of years. It must have been all the talk about Abigail's encounter with their sister's clone at the care center that had stirred up hibernating thoughts.

In the dream, Meese had come for a spectral visit, wearing the same radiant smile that had been the hallmark of her short life. Tracey now pressed her lids tightly together, willing a return to that place of joyful reunion, but could not retrieve the vision. She turned to her side, snuggled more deeply into the comforter, and murmured, "I love you, Meese."

Dale's snore was cut short as he snuffled himself to wakefulness. "Did you say something, Trace?"

Tracey's eyelids parted slightly. "Sorry, I didn't mean to wake you," she apologized.

"You okay?"

"Yeah," she sighed. "I just had a dream about Meese, that's all."

Dale slipped his arm beneath Tracey's head and pulled her closer. "You want to tell me about it?"

Tracey nestled in beside him, glad for the chance to relive her illusion. "I was walking into our dining room and saw Meese standing in the kitchen. We gave each other that look that said we both knew that she was only here in spirit, and only came to say hello. I kept my eyes focused on her face as I walked across the room, afraid that if I looked away, she would disappear. Meese held out her hand to me, smiling in a pleased way. So I went toward her and we walked into each others' arms. I remember thinking that this wasn't just a dream, it was actually Meese coming to see me." Tracey hesitated, and then asked tentatively, "Do you suppose it could have been real?"

Dale took a deep breath. "I think it's very likely. It may be that we too often discount, as just another dream, the visions we receive, when, in reality, there's an important message there for us."

Tracey nodded against Dale's shoulder and continued, "In my dream I focused on every detail, not wanting to forget any of it. I remember feeling Meese's love, and that she was proud of me and was there to let me know that I was doing okay. And then, while I was still hugging her, I felt her spirit leaving my arms."

Dale turned to face his wife, placing a kiss on her forehead. "You sure you're all right?"

"Um-hmm. In my dream, I wasn't sad at all. The hardest part is waking up and realizing, all over again, that she's really gone. Still, I'm so grateful for every time I get those visits, or whatever you want to call them, because I miss her so much." Tracey sighed heavily; then in a melancholy mood she rolled back the covers, and swung her feet to the floor, remaining on the edge of the bed, reluctant to begin her day.

96

Dale looked at the clock and groaned. "I guess I'd better get up, too. I probably need to clear the driveway before I leave for work. What are your plans for today?"

Tracey rubbed her hands across her face, as if to wipe away any evidence of sorrow that might remain there. "I have some sewing I need to do. Then I told Dad I'd take him shopping this morning. We'll probably stop for lunch and end up at his apartment, shoveling out the debris. I'll be home before dinner."

The day's prospective duties were not any that Tracey anticipated with pleasure, except maybe lunch. Her father's limited funds made gift buying a bedeviling chore. Melvin never had comprehended the value of things–or, at least not their cost. He had always considered his own possessions to be worth much more, and others' much less than was realistic. So, shopping with him unfailingly included an embarrassing barrage of his complaints, forcefully directed at the hapless clerks. He invariably did it with a smile, pretending graciousness, and expecting his self-perceived charm to assuage the hostile reaction of his victims. His harsh attacks notwithstanding, he was a pleaser, at all times desiring others' good will. But, more often than not, the two shoppers would depart the store minus the sought after purchases, not to mention any pleasant, "Have a good day"s.

Tracey and Abigail shared the weekly responsibility of keeping their dad's living quarters habitable, which consisted, along with the normal dusting and vacuuming, of discarding the weekly pileup of old newspapers, and rescuing dirty dishes from every conceivable resting place in the apartment: the floor beside the sofa, the back of the toilet, under the bed, behind the Lazy Boy–anywhere he felt disposed to ditch them. When Tracey visited her dad, she always felt like she'd just stepped into Hobo Heaven. She knew it was difficult for him to walk, so assumed that the effort needed to transport the remains of his meals to the kitchen sink was daunting. Her understanding of his debility, however, didn't alleviate her aversion to the necessary task of cleaning up the odorous results.

To all of the above, add Melvin's "in no uncertain terms" refusal to wear a hearing aid–his family members had to substantially increase the decibels of any attempt at conversation–and "life with Father" was hardly a re-enactment of the well-loved , if chimerical, 1953 television series.

The day unfolded as expected, and by the time Tracey returned home that evening, she was exhausted. This was her normal "visit Mom" night, but Tracey's supply of patience had been depleted for one day. She knew that others saw her as indefatigable, but she, nevertheless, did have her down times. Since Nadine probably wouldn't know whether she'd been there or not, she decided to delay the ritual for another twenty-four hours.

All things considered, it was perhaps a fortuitous decision. On that particular evening Nadine was in a positively foul temper. She had all the nurses rolling their eyes, only because any other action that came to mind could result in a law suit. Just before dinner she punched the CNA who came to push her wheelchair into the dining room. Nadine was not about to eat any more of the "crap they pass off as food in this place!" Those were not her *exact* words; the real ones were considerably more colorful than can be repeated in genteel company. For the past three years, as her inhibitions had become progressively tranquilized, her language had concurrently grown more offensive. A younger Nadine would have been outraged at such a display of vulgarity.

It was with a sigh of relief that the nurse finally administered her meds and settled her in for the night. Nadine was still asleep at eleven o'clock when the door opened and, once again, admitted the only person who knew how to unlock the chambers of her intellect. Lisa laid a light hand on the somnolent form. "Nadine, it's me. Are you awake?"

Nadine's slowly emerging smile was only a small indication of the joy she felt at the appearance of her sweet young confidant. "Oh, Lisa, I'm so glad you're here. Promise you'll never go away altogether."

Lisa smiled. "Never. I promise." She once again tilted up the head of the bed, pulled the chair close, and got comfortable for the narrative that she knew was forthcoming. "I believe you were telling me about your farm in Rigby."

Nadine took a deep breath. "I loved my country home. For the next few years we were almost completely self-reliant. Every spring we planted a huge garden, which the children, of course, deplored weeding. We raised our own meat, ground our own flour, milked our own cows, gathered our own eggs, and even learned to make our own cheese. In between times, we rode our horses, and visited friends. That was my age of contentment. I told Melvin that, when I died, I wanted to be buried in the back yard."

"And what did he say?"

"Oh, Melvin was pretty stodgy and conservative; he always took everything I said literally, so he figured he needed to tell me that there were ordinances against that sort of thing." Nadine huffed softly. "I was always expressing my random ideas, which were merely fanciful thinking, and he unfailingly took me at my word. I remember, after we got engaged, I told him one night that maybe we should just elope, and he immediately launched into this grand soliloquy about how we couldn't disappoint our parents that way, blah, blah, blah. Pff! I didn't really want to; I just thought it sounded daring and romantic. Anyway, where was I?"

"Your country home."

"Oh, yes. What a beautiful little farm we had there." Nadine's countenance became almost beatific as she reminisced silently for a few moments. Then, suddenly aware that she had retreated into her own thoughts while Lisa waited expectantly, she continued, "One of Tracey's favorite tricks was to change the clock in Abby's room, and then wake her in the middle of the night to tell her it was time to get up for school. Poor Abby would be all dressed and heading down to breakfast before she realized that she'd only just barely gone to bed.

Lisa tried to suppress a grin as she insincerely commiserated, "Poor Abby. It's bad enough getting up when you have to!"

"Oh, Tracey was always up to something. She was the mischievous one; Abby was always more serious. She did do something once that surprised me, though, considering her non- frivolous nature. When she was a sophomore in high school, a request was made for participants in the Jefferson County Rodeo Queen contest. She responded to the call, in spite of the fact that she had never taken horseback riding seriously. Our bishop loaned her his Appaloosa because our own horses were not well seasoned, and each day I would accompany her to a neighbor's backyard arena, where my friend gave her a modicum of training and then allowed her to stay for as long as she wanted to practice.

"Returning home one afternoon my mare got spooked and took off unexpectedly at a full-out run. I wasn't prepared for the sudden jolt of G-force, lost my balance, and slowly began slipping off the saddle as I tried desperately to halt the mare's progress. Abby was several yards in front, moving along at a swift gallop, and couldn't hear my frantic yelling. I just kept sliding more and more to one side, so, since I wasn't able to regain my seat, I finally decided that the smartest move would be to release my white-knuckled grip on the saddle horn and let myself fall ignominiously to the ground. The next thing I remember is standing and brushing off my pants. That's when I noticed that a couple of neighbors, the Flynn brothers, who'd happened along just at that moment, were reigning in my crazed mount so that I could continue my ride home."

"Were you hurt?" asked Lisa.

"I had a split lip and a bruised cheek, but the most serious damage sustained was to my pride."

"So, did you keep on riding after that?"

"Oh, yes. It wasn't the first time I'd been thrown, nor was it the last. Just before Abby got married, she and Barry went with us on a trail ride up Table Rock. It was a pretty strenuous climb, but when we got to the top, the view was amazing. It looked like you could reach out your hand and touch the Granddady Teton. Melvin took a whole roll of film, and then, when we got home, discovered that the end hadn't latched onto the spool, so he didn't have one picture."

"Oh, how disappointing."

"Yes, especially since we never made that ride again. Anyway, when we stopped there on the top of the mountain, Melvin noticed that my saddle had loosened up and was slipping to one side, so he dismounted and, playing the macho cowboy, redid the cinch with a vengeance. Consequently, on the way back down the trail, suddenly my horse's head lowered, his front legs buckled, and he rolled over onto one side. I was able to jump clear, but then Melvin and I just stood there with our mouths open and our wits hanging out, wondering what was wrong, while the poor beast lay there, wide-eyed and panting. If it hadn't been for Barry, the miserable animal would have, no doubt, died on the spot.

However, our future son-in-law had the sense to come running and immediately flip loose the saddle cinch. As I said before, we were pretty ignorant when it came to horses, even after all that time of owning them; this was a few years after Abby's rodeo queen adventure.

"And how did Abby do in that?"

"Well, she didn't win—most of the contestants had begun riding almost before they could walk—but we had a wonderful time preparing her for the event. And, even though she was inexperienced, she performed very well. Also, while she may not have been the most accomplished, she was by far the prettiest."

"Was that when the situation between the two of you improved?"

"Not really. Our reconciliation, if that's what you want to call it, happened when she was a senior in high school and began dating a boy of less than sterling character. Tracey, at the same time, was interested in his brother, but was, of course, too young yet to date, so she used to sneak behind our backs to be with him. But I'm getting sidetracked again. Abby's relationship with this boy was getting quite serious, even though she knew, deep down, that he wasn't right for her.

"She finally came to her senses and tried to break it off. That's when he became physical and started knocking her around." Lisa gasped when she heard this, and Nadine nodded for emphasis. "Every time she tried to get away from him, he became abusive. Finally she decided that she needed my help. We stayed up all night, one night, while she told me everything that was going on. And, in some miraculous way, during those hours of shared confidences, Abby and I became best friends"

Lisa's eyes dropped to the floor as she sat, musing. "So that's what happened," she murmured to herself.

"Hmm?"

"What happened to the boyfriend?"

"We got a restraining order, which helped temporarily. Of course, she still saw him at school, but he never dared to attack her there. Not long after that his family moved away, so that was the welcome end of the problem."

"Interesting how sometimes the smallest thing can have such a huge impact," Lisa reflected. "Not that Abby getting knocked around was insignificant, but the fact that she turned to you for help. That was all you needed to draw the two of you close. Out of small and simple things . . . ."

"I always loved her. We just had a hard time getting along–until that happened. Like you said, I was probably jealous. In later years, Abby would say things to me like, 'That was back when you hated me.'" Nadine shook her head sadly. "It broke my heart that she had suffered for years under that misconception.

"I was never abusive in any way; it wasn't that. It was just that I spent so much time trying to make my children do everything perfectly, there was no time to show them how proud I was of the perfect things they were already doing.

"Tracey was another one who believed, for a long time, that I didn't like her. How could I have failed so miserably at the single most important duty of motherhood?" She studied Lisa's face for a long moment, as if hoping to find absolution there, but the nurse's expression was inscrutable. Nadine took a deep breath and puffed it out. "I don't know how my boys felt–they've always been a bit reticent–or if Meese perceived me the same as the other two girls. Children don't always express their innermost feelings until they get older, at least not to their parents.

"Long after Tracey became an adult, she finally opened up and told me how she'd always felt, which gave me the chance to dispel some of her false beliefs. But Meese didn't live long enough to reach the stage of disclosure." Nadine's eyes glistened with spilling tears as she lowered her lids. "You know, you never really get over grieving the loss of a child; you just learn to deal with the pain."

Lisa leaned forward to brush back a strand of hair that had fallen across Nadine's forehead. "I'm so sorry."

The old woman lifted her eyes and wiped the back of one hand across her cheek. "Oh, but I wouldn't want it any other way. I hope I never forget the unbearable heartache; to be completely free of the pain would be to somehow diminish Meese's worth. If I forget the sorrow, then I might also forget the love. I only wish I'd told her more often."

"But she knows now," Lisa stated confidently.

"I suppose she does, but I should've said it to all of them, every day. I should have told them what great kids they were, and are. In my childhood home, praise was severely rationed, and the "L" word was never spoken, so I guess I didn't think it was important. I assumed they knew without me articulating the words. I was wrong."

Lisa smiled. "Another lesson learned."

"Yes, but too late!" cried Nadine. "Always too late!"

"You're mistaken, you know; it's never too late," Lisa contradicted. "Besides, you need to give your children some credit. When they became parents, a whole new vista would have opened up to them. They may still criticize now and then, but they understand, and they forgive."

Nadine again wiped her eyes as the beginning of a smile flickered across her lips. "I remember once, when Tracey's children were young, she told me that she remembered, as a little girl, doing some of the same things that her own kids were now doing, and it became suddenly clear to her why those things had annoyed me so much."

"You see? With added maturity comes increased"–Lisa grinned–"perspicacity." She gave a short titter at the old woman's startled expression, which quickly turned to one of mischief.

"I see that you can be quite loquacious," Nadine observed with a twinkle in her eye.

Lisa immediately picked up the challenge. "Only when it's efficacious," she countered, getting into the spirit of the game.

"And not just to be braggadocios?"

"Never!" Lisa objected. "But possibly, on occasion, pugnacious."

"What about supercilious?"

"How could you even suggest it?" teased Lisa. "I'm really very unpretentious."

They were, by this time, giggling like a couple of school girls. "And very bodacious!" hooted Nadine.

"I think," Lisa chortled, "that we're both quite splendiferous."

Nadine couldn't remember the last time she had laughed so hard. "Stop!" she cried. "You're making my stomach hurt."

Lisa's merriment gradually subsided, and she asked, "So, what about Tracey? What happened between her and the brother she was sneaking out to meet?"

Nadine sighed. "They were in love, which caused me no end of panic and sleepless nights. Tracey thought I objected to their romance because I didn't like the boy. She had always, from the time she was in junior high, accused me of being judgmental. But there's a difference, you know, between making judgments and being judgmental. We have to discriminate, every day, between what is good for us and what will only bring us sorrow.

"The thing is, I did like him; I just didn't like some of the choices he was making, and worried that they would impact my daughter in detrimental ways. But, when a child is that age, and that determined, there's not much a parent can do.

"I actually caught her in a lie once, when she was going out to meet him. It broke my heart that she would try to deceive me; Tracey had never before acted in wilful defiance. She was the one who was always apologizing and trying to make everyone happy, unlike Abby, who quietly had a mind of her own. Meese was somewhere in between.

"Sometimes being overly eager to please, though, is not such a good thing. It can make you too vulnerable to others' questionable objectives. It's perhaps better to be a little bit stubborn and noncompliant." Nadine sighed. "If Tracey hadn't been such a pleaser, maybe she could have avoided a good many of the pitfalls that plagued her.

"It was in December of that same year that a hypnotist was invited to the school to put on a show. During the afternoon assembly Tracey volunteered to be one of his subjects–one of his *best* subjects, as it turned out. At that time I didn't realize that it was possible for her to be so manipulated, but she completely surrendered her will to that shaman.

"After school, when she told me that she had participated in his antics, I strictly forbade her to return that evening for his encore performance–I did not feel good about the whole matter. The next thing I knew, there was Tracey in her boyfriend's car, heading down the road on the way back to the school. I later learned that, during the afternoon show, he had given her a post-hypnotic suggestion to return for his evening appearance.

"Melvin and I had gone to a company party that night, and when we returned home, several of our neighbors were in front of our garage, waiting for us. Tracey had been taken to the hospital as a result of her evening exhibition. Actually, it turned out to be a case of vestibulitis, but the gyrations which the hypnotist had put her through had severely exacerbated the problem.

"I've always believed that hypnotism can be very dangerous when used as a parlor game, and I was livid that the school had brought in that kind of show. I telephoned and told them how outraged I was over the caliber of entertainment that they considered to be appropriate for high school kids, but of course, it was all after the fact, so what good did it do?

"Tracey recovered after about a week, and evidently had learned her lesson. To my knowledge, she hasn't, since that time, exposed herself to any similar embarrassment."

"Embarrassment?"

"Oh, yes. As I understand it, her hypnotic performance commenced with some rather energetic dance routines, including a few bumps and grinds, and culminated with her down on all fours, throwing up long strings of spaghetti, which she'd had for dinner, all the while persisting in her frenzied acrobatics."

"Embarrassment!"

Nadine nodded ruefully. "Now, as far as her boyfriend was concerned, she finally realized that she had better options and broke up with him just before he moved away. I was never so relieved as when that family left the neighborhood."

"And your daughters are happily married now?"

"I believe so. It took Tracey a few hard lumps before she finally found what she was looking for, but Dale is a good man, and treats her well, as far as I know. Abby and Barry met a couple of years after college and seem to be made for each other. Both of my girls are grandmothers now, a few times over. And they're still best friends."

CHAPTER 8 - *Tuesday, December 21ˢᵗ*

Each year on Danny's birthday, Abigail and Tracey met for lunch at Café Rio, and in honor of their little brother, indulged in his favorite food. The culinary choice was no hardship on their taste buds; both sisters claimed that, if their preference in cuisine was any indication, there must have been a Mexican in the woodpile somewhere along the ancestral line.

Abigail was already at the restaurant when Tracey came blustering in. "Sorry I'm late," she apologized. "I didn't realize the roads were so bad."

Abigail glanced at her watch as she stood. "I'm still okay with the time. I don't have to be back until one-thirty."

They joined the end of the line and slowly made their way toward the preparation counter. There was never any discussion over their choice of menu item. Danny had been addicted to sweet pork burritos, and they felt it their privilege and pleasure to carry on his tradition. "How many of these things do you suppose he consumed before he left for Iraq?" Abigail asked as she placed her meal on the table and lowered herself into a chair.

"Well, let's see." Tracey sat and unwrapped her plastic fork. "If you figure he started when he was twelve and averaged three or four a week until he was nineteen–man, if he could have stored up all that fuel, he could have launched himself to the moon."

"Tracey!" Abigail pretended offense, but was, as always, privately amused by her sister's unrestrained mouth. Still grinning, she lifted her glass of Sprite. "To Danny," she toasted. "May he join us here next year."

Tracey raised her glass and clinked it against Abigail's. "And then maybe you and I can start checking out the other items on the menu!"

They each took a sip, returned their drinks to the table, and switched their attention to the entrees before them, while each of their thoughts meandered back through time. Then Tracey laughed. "I remember, when Danny was about a year old, I used to make him cry on purpose, just so I could love him better."

"You always did have a warped sense of decorum," observed Abigail. Tracey chortled her acknowledgment of the fact, and her sister continued, "I'm thinking of the time, right after we moved to Rigby, when you hid from Mom out in the trees behind our house. She was nearly frantic by the time she found you."

Tracey quirked up her mouth. "I know. I just thought I was being funny; it never occurred to me how panicked Mom would be. But I'm surprised you remember it."

"Of course I do. You had me scared to death, as well, especially since you'd already tried to drown yourself in the canal, over at the other house."

"That was years before. I wasn't three anymore."

"No, but you were still young enough to drown. The canal there was a lot bigger than the one in Idaho Falls."

110

"Poor Mom. She's had to weather a lot of storms, hasn't she?" She gave her sister a solemn look. "Do you really think Danny'll ever come home, Ab?"

"I think, as long as there's no evidence to the contrary, there's still hope. Stranger things have happened."

"But in your heart of hearts," Tracey relentlessly probed, "what do you really believe?"

Abigail lowered her eyes. "I believe that I can't bear the thought of never seeing him again in this life. But I also believe that, considering what he might be going through, he may be better off dead. So I believe that it's best not to consider the probabilities."

Tracey sighed. "Yeah, me too."

Abigail turned to her meal, but was soon aware that her sister was absently stabbing her fork into her own burrito, as if assaulting a voodoo doll. "Trace?"

Tracey lifted her head. "Sorry. I was just wondering why our family has had so much adversity. First Meese, then Danny, and now Mom. There ought to be a limit, don't you think?"

Abigail gave her sister a quirky look. "You're not usually one to ask, 'Why me?'"

"I know. I just think about it now and then."

"Is everything okay with you, Trace?"

"You mean, do I have cancer or something?" She snorted and shook her head. "Everything's fine. I guess I'm just having one of my reflective moments."

"I didn't know you had any," Abigail teased, although she knew better. There wasn't much that the sisters kept from each other, and Abigail understood that even light-hearted Tracey had occasional moments of serious thought.

"December's always hard, isn't it?" Tracey explained. "How ironic is it that both of our absent sibs were born during this month?"

"Yeah, but really how fitting," countered Abigail, "since they were both so Christlike." She smiled. "That's what we need to dwell on."

"Well, listen to you with the platitudes," declared Tracey churlishly. Then, at Abigail's injured look, she apologized. "I'm sorry, that sorta popped out. No offense meant. I guess I'm just in the mood for a pity party. I don't feel like looking on the bright side; I want to wallow in my sorrow."

"That's not like you."

"I think it started with a dream I had about Meese a couple of nights ago. You know how hard it is when you wake up and realize, all over again, that she really did die, and that it's going to be a long time before we see her again?" Tracey clenched her teeth. "Ooooh! Whenever I think about it, I just have this terrible urge to hit something. It's not fair, Ab. I want her back!" She shook her head dolefully. "I just want her back." She took a deep breath, and whuffed it out.

"Then Dad kind of set me off when I took him shopping yesterday. I swear he gets worse every year with the insults and demands. You know what? I don't like being a parent to my parents."

"Well, it's nice to know that you're human, after all," Abigail observed. "You know, sometimes I just wish that—"

Tracey eyed her sister inquisitively. "You just wish that what?"

Abigail shook her head. "I shouldn't even say it out loud."

"You wish that what?" persisted Tracey.

Abigail stared into her sister's eyes, wondering if she dared admit her selfish thoughts. "I just wish there were an end to it."

"It? You mean Mom?"

Abigail nodded, shamefaced, and Tracey smiled in understanding. "Do you know how many times I've thought that very same thing?"

"You? But you always seem to handle it like it's no big deal, the way you've always handled everything."

"Oh, my gosh, if you only knew! I guess we're *both* human, huh? But," she slapped her palm against the table top, "enough of this!" She again lifted her glass. "Another toast," she proposed. "To happy thoughts and loving memories, and someday, joyful reunions."

Abigail tipped her glass against Tracey's. "And, on that note, I will bid you adieu. I'd better get back to work before they discover they can get along without me." The sisters stood and hugged. "I love you, Trace. I'm glad we've at least got each other."

Tracey nodded. "Likewise, Sis."

That afternoon, for Nadine, was just like any other: long hours of confusion interspersed with periods of angst. But, with the change of shifts that night, came also her realization of the significance of this particular square on the calendar. "This is a special day, Lisa," Nadine announced at the appearance of her little friend.

"Oh? Someone's birthday maybe?"

"I think you must be psychic." Nadine paused and gave Lisa a wistful look. "It's Danny's birthday."

Lisa pulled her chair up to the bed and sat, leaning forward. "So, tell me about Danny. Was he another perfect child?"

Nadine chuckled. "Not really, but he was so charming he had everyone believing he was." She pressed her lips together and sighed. "Danny was someone special. He had a lot of difficulties when he was born, but his little spirit was strong; he was a fighter. He overcame all of his health problems and grew into a sturdy little boy. When he was three or four we constantly put him on exhibition to our friends by

113

requesting that he show off his muscles. And he really had them! He would invariably roll his eyes and then grudgingly oblige; I'm sure he was thinking, 'Not again!'

"In spite of his intrinsic reluctance to show off, when he got older he competed in the 'Mr. Utah' bodybuilding contest and took fourth place in the teen-age division. I took great pride in displaying his competition photos to all of my friends." She laughed. "One of them told me, 'You shouldn't show these pictures to single ladies like me!'"

Nadine fluttered her hands. "But I'm getting ahead of my story. In second grade Danny began wrestling on the school team, and I think it was only a year later that he signed up for 'Grid Kid' football. He wasn't very big, but he was mighty determined. He put his whole heart into his sport, just as he did everything. As a little kid he was such a scrapper, the football coach had him playing on both the offensive and defensive squads, and his teammates, when they were in a crunch, would always beg, 'Send Danny in.'

"Melvin and I never missed a match or a game for as long as he participated. Danny was twice voted MVP on his high school wrestling team, took first place in region one year, and was team captain when he was a senior. He was a real champion, inside and out.

"Then, when all of the disturbance erupted in the middle east, Danny, of course, felt it his duty to join in the conflict. On the one hand I was so proud of him, but at the same time it nearly tore my heart out to see him go off to battle." Nadine's face clouded. "People with tender hearts like Danny should never be exposed to the vileness of war." She huffed. "Nobody should. But, even in the scriptures are countless references to that which is most loathsome of all that is criminal: man's inhumanity to man. I hate that the world is so depraved, and that my children and grandchildren are daily subjected to its corruption, Danny most of all.

"He faithfully kept in touch, and his letters were the sweetest you can imagine. We'd call the other kids to come over whenever one arrived, and we'd read it together. He never failed to express his love and appreciation for us, his family. He told us affectionate things that boys don't usually verbalize to their parents. And, of course, he always included a good-natured little jab at Tracey, who had always doted on him.

"Then, one day, three uniformed men came to our door." Nadine paused. "You know, during World War II, a lot of war films were made, and they always had a scene where a wife or mother or sweetheart would receive the dreaded telegram. No one had to be told its contents; a wire was always the worst kind of news: a son or husband dead or missing. Sometimes the woman would faint before she even read it.

"But, the actuality of a mother's heartbreak is unimaginable to anyone who hasn't experienced it. Danny—my little freckle-faced Danny—was reported missing in action. And that's how his status has remained. We still don't know what's happened to him."

Lisa was deep in thought. "I have connections in some pretty high places," she said. "Why don't I see what I can find out?"

Nadine smiled sorrowfully. "You're welcome to try, Sweetie, but I don't know what you can do."

Lisa shrugged. "You never know. I have a brother who's a very powerful man. He just may exert some influence where it matters. At least, it's worth a try. But tell me about when Danny was born. You said he had some problems."

"That was a difficult time," Nadine reflected, "but first let me tell you another little story that happened several months before." She shifted on the bed, seeking a more comfortable position. "Tracey was nearing high school graduation when I found out I was pregnant. Abby was in college, but had wangled a job at Yellowstone Park for the summer, and was very proud of herself and excited to start.

"As soon as school was out, Meese was to drive her sister to Wyoming and then return home to look for a job of her own. The two of them took their dad's pickup and headed out, but on the way there the truck broke down, so Melvin had to drive my car up and rescue them. They managed to deliver Abby to her destination, but on the way home Melvin predictably made a wrong turn and he and Meese ended up in Bozeman, Montana. By this time they were long overdue, and without the modern convenience of cell phones, I had no way of knowing what had happened. There I was, panicked and pregnant: not a good combination." Nadine chuckled. "Melvin never could follow a map, and wouldn't bother reading road signs. It wasn't until they invented the GPS that I quit wondering, every time he left the house, if he'd find his way back again."

Lisa laughed and nodded her head. "What did you do about the truck?"

"You know, I can't remember. It seems like our cars were always breaking down in those days. We couldn't afford to buy anything dependable. I suppose Melvin arranged to have it repaired in whatever town it was, and then we must have gone up to get it. I don't know if I went along to drive one of the vehicles home, or if it was one of the children. Come to think of it, it was probably Jimmy or one of the girls; I was so miserably ill with my pregnancy, all I wanted to do was lie in bed and groan.

"I had a feeling that something was wrong with the baby. I don't know why; the doctor kept assuring me that all was as it should be. But

I instinctively knew different and secretly shed many tears because of it. As it turns out, Abby also knew. She told me years later that, when we first announced the pregnancy to our children, the thought came to her that there would be some serious difficulties.

"She was surprised when Melvin called from the hospital to say that Danny had been born and all was well. Of course, it really wasn't; he just hadn't been informed yet. Danny had refused to be delivered in the normal way, so an emergency C-section was necessary. The doctor didn't tell me until I was back in my room that my baby had life-threatening respiratory and gastro-intestinal disorders. It took me two days to muster up the courage to walk down to the nursery to visit him. I knew he was hooked up to all kinds of wires and tubes and it scared me to think about seeing him in that condition.

"It turned out to be a sweet experience, though. The nurse pulled him out of the isolette so that I could hold him, and I noticed that, each time I kissed him, his monitor showed an increase in his heart rate." Nadine chuckled pensively. "It just proves that, right from birth, people respond to love.

"I was discharged four days later, on Christmas Day, but had to leave my newborn in the hospital. The family had waited to open presents until I arrived, but the idea of celebrating was repugnant to me. Nevertheless, I put on my best face and tried to enjoy their enthusiasm.

"Because of the C-section I couldn't stand up straight for a week; after all, I was forty-two years old, not exactly in my prime. Danny stayed in the hospital for ten days, and even after we brought him home it was touch and go for quite a while. I never thought I'd survive all the stress, but here I am."

"I think we should celebrate his birthday," suggested Lisa. "After all, he was something of a miracle baby." She grimaced. "Too bad I didn't bring a cake."

Nadine's eyebrows lifted. "Actually, I'd rather have ice cream."

Lisa grinned collusively. "I think I can manage that, if you don't mind me slipping out for a few minutes. Any special orders?"

"I've always loved cherry chocolate chip concretes from Nielsen's. But it's way too late; they'll be closed by now."

A sparkle came into Lisa's eyes. "You're not going to believe this, but my family happens to know the owner. I think he'd be willing to do a favor for his friends."

"You're going to wake him in the middle of the night?"

"I promise, he won't mind in the least."

"There's another problem," Nadine complained. "I don't have any money."

Lisa stood and patted Nadine on the hand. "This will be my treat." She smoothed Nadine's covers and fluffed her pillows, then moved toward the door. "I'll be as quick as I can, so don't go anywhere," she teased.

Nadine smiled to herself. She hadn't been this naughty in many a year. Lisa had a way of making her feel young, like her former self. She sighed pensively. Too bad you can't pick out all of the happy moments in your life and relive them. She'd never been one to say, "If I had it to do over again. . . ." She realized that, with a few exceptions, she'd probably have done things exactly the same way the second time around. Her regrets notwithstanding, she was who she was.

No, she didn't want to go back and change things; she just wanted the pleasure of repeating the good times. Memories were fine, but they didn't compare to the real thing. She wanted to live again in her childhood home, and make mud pies with her best friend next door. She wanted to hear her daddy tell one of his slightly off-color jokes and then laugh harder than anyone. She wanted to go out on her first date again, and cheer for her high school football team, and perform with her friends in three-act plays at church. She'd like to relive the late forties, after the war, when all she could imagine for her future were light-hearted days and happy endings.

She huffed softly to herself. One thing she'd learned over the years: real life stories seldom ended all neatly bundled up and tied with a ribbon, each loose end tidily tucked inside. Children strayed, love disappointed, friends lost touch, aspirations failed. The important thing was to maintain hope, to keep believing that it was all worth it, and that someday it would be okay.

She'd forever been a dreamer, looking toward tomorrow; "Over the Rainbow" could have been her theme song. Next year was always going to be better than this one, with more money, more time, more opportunities. Even into her sixties she'd still imagined that there were better days ahead.

Then, all at once, had come the abrupt realization that all of her tomorrows were destined to be just like her todays. No more camp-outs or automobile trips, the car packed with diapers and baby beds. No more happy expectations about a new school year, a new love interest, a new home, a new adventure. No more curiosity about what exploits might lie in wait around life's next bend; the road from there on would be straight and predictable. Her daddy had always said that "anticipation is better than realization." As a child, she wasn't sure that she believed him, but with the passing of years, she'd been forced to acknowledge that it was, indeed, true. Of all the things that she'd had to relinquish as she got older, the prospect of new experiences had been the most difficult to surrender.

If only she could go back to the time when she was surrounded by all of her children, before Tracey had chosen to strike out on her own, and while Meese and Danny were still around. How she wished that they could all be together once more: the whole family. Well, she sighed, too late for that.

Her thoughts were interrupted as Lisa breezed in through the door, carrying a container heaped with ice cream. "That didn't take you long," Nadine noted.

"I didn't have to go far," replied Lisa. She handed Nadine her cup and again settled into the chair beside the bed. "You can't start eating, though, until we sing 'Happy Birthday' to Danny."

Blending their voices, they gave a fair-to-middling rendition of the number, with Nadine changing to a harmony part for the last few bars. They then looked at each other and began to giggle, magically dissipating the difference in their ages. "Okay," Lisa declared, "in between bites you have to go on with the story. I don't think you finished telling me about when Danny was born."

"Well, like I said, he was a pretty sick baby for awhile." Nadine took a spoonful of her frozen treat, savoring the delectable flavor. She then began to chuckle. "When he was a couple of weeks old, my friend Vaudis came up from Utah to give me moral support and any help she could offer. She brought along Jon, her little three-year-old, and we put up a couple of cots for them in the living room. On the first night they were there, Jon wanted to know why his mother was sleeping in the same room with him. Vaudis asked, 'Where do you think I should sleep?' Jon looked at her like the answer to that was obvious. 'In with Mr. and Mrs. Collins!'"

Lisa smiled. "It takes a pretty good friend to come all that way to help out."

"You don't have to tell me; she's always been the best. She stayed a whole week, and it was so nice having some adult company; as long as she was there I felt like I wasn't completely isolated from the outside world. I don't think we did a single thing but visit; we could always find something to talk about.

"I was pretty much tied to the house with Danny, but I remember how badly I wanted to have that family portrait done. I was so afraid that he would die before we got a picture of all of us together. But, like I said, I just couldn't manage to get the arrangements made."

"Did you ever just come right out and ask someone to take care of it for you?" Lisa sensibly wondered.

Nadine grimaced. "No. That was one of my little idiosyncracies. I always imagined that the people close to me should be able to notice what needed to be done, without my specifically pointing it out, and then just do it because they loved me. Never did happen, though."

"Sounds like you may have had some pride issues," Lisa chided.

Nadine grinned sheepishly. "Ya think? Anyway," she sighed, "as it turned out, it wasn't Danny who died; it was Meese." Nadine took another deep breath. "Oh my, but I miss my little girl."

"I'm sure she's missed you, too," Lisa offered quietly.

"I've heard it said that those who pass on experience the same grief at parting as we who are left behind. Do you suppose that's true?"

"Why wouldn't they?" reasoned Lisa. "Emotions don't die with the body, they live with the spirit. Those who have gone on care deeply about their loved ones who are still on the earth, especially family members. I'm pretty sure your Meese is doing everything she can to help you and your family through the hard times." She pointed to

Nadine's ice cream cup, which the old woman had miraculously emptied while she spoke. "I'll take that and throw it away. It's about time you got some sleep. They'll soon be coming to get you for breakfast."

Nadine let out a short titter. "I just had my breakfast."

CHAPTER 9 - *Wednesday, December 22nd*

The next day Abigail was still contemplating her possible decline into premature dementia, when her cell phone rang. It was Tracey. "Okay, I've been thinking that it's time I got serious about finding that nurse; we need to talk to her directly. I wonder if she's still working the night shift. Are you up to a midnight meeting?"

"So, you believe now that I didn't dream the whole thing?"

"Well, since you're so sure about it, I think it's time we find out, once and for all. I'll pick you up at eleven forty-five."

The rest of the day slogged along, giving Abigail no end of trouble concentrating on the tasks at hand. The possibility of finally uncovering the truth about her mom and this nurse, Lisa, kept her keyed up to the point of total distraction. After several of her coworkers made remarks about her uncharacteristic lack of focus, she decided that she may as well leave her office early. She still had a good amount of house cleaning to do before Jimmy and Marlene arrived the next day. At least her mind needn't be engaged while she changed beds and scrubbed toilets.

By nine o'clock the house was in sparkling good order, so she kicked back in the recliner and flipped on the TV. Because Barry was in his office, finishing up some work he'd brought home, she punched in the numbers for TCM, and was gratified to note that they were showing an old chick flick, "An Affair To Remember." She still got goose bumps when she thought of that scene where Cary Grant discovers that Deborah Kerr is crippled. Did real-live men ever look at a woman that way?

The movie ended at 10:15, leaving her in tears, as always. With an hour and a half to kill, she picked up the book she was reading and soon became engrossed in the story of two brothers who were so totally devoted to each other that, even when one of them died, he refused to move on to the afterlife. Each evening, at sundown, he would return to hang out with his older brother, playing catch and swimming in the lake.

"If only we had that choice," murmured Abigail wistfully. She'd give anything if Meese could return each evening, not necessarily to play catch or swim, but just so she could see her, and talk to her, and once again put her arms around her and breathe in the essence that was exclusively "Meese."

She was forced from her reverie when Tracey arrived to pick her up, on time even–possibly a first. "So, are you ready for this?" her sister asked as they climbed into the car.

"I'm sick to my stomach, if that's what you mean," groaned Abigail. "What if I did imagine all of it? They say that Alzheimer's runs in families." She grimaced and Tracey laughed. "I'm serious, Trace. What if I'm going 'round the bend?"

Tracey rested a hand on Abigail's knee. "I'd be the first to tell you, Sis," she teased.

Abigail snorted. "I'm sure you would!"

The main doors to the care center were locked down at 10:00 P.M., so the two women drove to the side of the building, walked to the entrance, and punched in the code. Things were quiet inside; the hall was free of its daytime wheelchair lineup, along with the continual pleas for help from its occupants.

They approached Nadine's closed door and quietly rapped. From inside there came the sound of a scooting chair and muffled steps. The heavy door was opened and there stood–if they hadn't known better–their sister Meese. Tracey was stunned. Not only did she exist, but Abigail's description had been, if anything, understated.

Lisa smiled in welcome. "Come on in. We were just talking about you."

Abigail looked at Tracey as if to say, "I told you so!" but Tracey merely shrugged.

As they approached their mother's bed, Nadine's lids were closed; she appeared to be asleep. "Mom?" ventured Tracey. There was no response.

"Mom?" Abigail gave it a try. Nadine's eyes flickered open. She scowled a look at her daughters, then turned away and pulled the covers over her head. Abigail turned to the nurse. "I thought you said you'd been talking."

Lisa shrugged. "She's in and out." She turned to Tracey. "Tracey, I'm so glad you came tonight. I've been hoping you would."

Tracey gave her a skeptical look. "And you know me how?"

"There's no great mystery," Lisa assured her. "Your mom and I talk whenever she's feeling up to it. She's told me so much about all of you, I feel like a member of the family."

Tracey smirked. "Evidently a very privileged member. If what you say is true, you're the only one fortunate enough to see her as anything other than confused and angry."

Lisa smiled. "Don't give up hope. I'm sure you'll eventually catch her on a good day, or night, as the case may be."

"No one else seems to think so," Abigail countered. "Everyone here tells us that it can't happen."

Lisa shrugged. "Doctors and nurses don't know everything. Alzheimer's is still pretty much of an enigma."

"I guess we'll have to take your word for it," Tracey remonstrated, "since you're the sole witness." She paused, and stared almost accusingly at Lisa, completely disconcerted by the nurse's resemblance to Meese.

"Is something wrong?" asked Lisa. "You're kinda creeping me out."

Tracey shook her head. "Sorry, it's just that you look so much like our sister."

Lisa chuckled. "That's what I understand. They say everyone has a twin somewhere."

"In your case it's more like a clone. You weren't conceived in a laboratory, were you?"

"Tracey!" cautioned Abigail, but Lisa was laughing.

"Your mom warned me that you say what's on your mind. But I assure you, I came into being by normal means."

"Are you from around here?" questioned Abigail.

"No," Lisa replied. "I'm just here temporarily; I'll soon be going home. I'm sorry your mother is being reclusive tonight. But don't give up."

The two sisters, after making one more attempt with Nadine, and receiving the usual rebuff, spoke their farewells and retreated toward the parking lot. "At least we know she's not a figment of your imagination," consoled Tracey as they pushed through the outside doorway. "But it would be a miracle if Mom had actually talked to her sensibly."

Abigail looked back at the dimly lit window to her mother's room. "Well, miracles do happen, you know."

At Nadine's bedside Lisa sat musing, her lower lip pulled in between her teeth. She looked at Nadine tentatively. "I just had a great idea," she announced. "At least *I* think it's a great idea." At this Nadine rolled her head toward Lisa, interest showing clearly on her features. Lisa continued, "Why don't we have a Christmas Eve party? Jimmy will be in town, so all of your children could come."

"Jimmy," murmured Nadine. "Are you sure he'll be here? I haven't seen him for so long." She shook her head. "I pity oldest children; they're the Guinea pigs in so many ways. Have I told you about the time I left him home with the girls while I ran an errand? Another one of those regrettable memories."

"I don't think so."

"He must have been eleven or so. I wasn't gone long, but when I returned, he was with a bunch of the Boy Scouts in the back of a pickup that was just pulling up to the front curb. They were heading out on a camping trip, and he had forgotten something and had to swing back by the house. In the first place, I had known nothing about the event, and in the second, he had left his sisters alone and taken off. I was so angry I yelled at him and told him he wasn't going anywhere! I made him unload his stuff and come back into the house. I'm sure he was mortified in front of his friends. What a terrible thing for me to do! I've regretted it ever since."

"But he had acted irresponsibly."

"He was eleven years old! I know he needed reprimanding, but it should have been done in a more gentle way. I had a habit of immediately flying off the handle instead of considering the best way to deal with uncomfortable situations."

"And, as a result, Jimmy then turned to a life of crime."

Nadine snorted. "No, of course not."

"We've had this conversation before, Nadine. It's time to rid yourself of old guilt. What matters isn't so much what you have or haven't done, as who you've become in the process. Remember, the Lord looks upon the heart. So let's keep happy thoughts, and concentrate on the Christmas party. Besides, I think I'll have a little surprise for you."

Nadine's countenance brightened. "I love surprises! What is it?"

Lisa cocked one eyebrow. "You know better than that! Didn't I just say it was a surprise? But, I'll give you a hint. It's something you've been wanting for a long time."

"Oh, now I'm really curious! How about another hint?"

"Oh, no you don't. You'll just have to wait until Christmas Eve. I'm sure, if I called Abby, she would be willing to arrange everything. What do you think?"

"I think I'm all for it, but will I have my wits about me so I can do more than just sit here and grouse?"

"Oh, now, you've never been one to poop out on a party, have you? I think it will be just the thing to keep you 'bright eyed and bushy tailed.'"

Nadine smirked mischievously. "Pig in a pan, Lisa; pig in a pan."

CHAPTER 10 - *Thursday, December 23ʳᵈ*

Jimmy and Marlene relaxed against their seats aboard flight 683 to Salt Lake City. "It'll be nice to see your family again," noted Marlene.

Jimmy nodded. "It's been awhile."

Marlene studied her husband's features, noticed the deep worry lines, and wondered if he was contemplating the subject that was uppermost in her own mind. She wanted to comfort him, but wasn't exactly sure what words to use. Finally, she decided to broach the topic head-on. "You know that your mom won't recognize you. Nothing's changed since the last time you saw her, except that she may be worse."

Jimmy glanced quickly in her direction, marveling at how well she had read his thoughts, then faced forward and nodded silently. He shouldn't have been surprised at his wife's intuition. She'd always sensed when something was bothering him, and usually could guess the source of his discontent.

They had met when Marlene hired on at the same company where Jimmy was already employed, and both had felt an immediate attraction. She was tall, nearly attaining Jimmy's six foot stature, and slim, with sandy hair and a fair complexion. By all appearances, they could have been brother and sister.

Though they'd never achieved parenthood (much to their disappointment), their lives were full and productive. In addition to his job as a manufacturing engineer, Jimmy tutored struggling high school students in math and science. It had taken him a long while to overcome the bitterness of infertility, but eventually he had displaced his desire for children of his own with a fervent zeal for helping the children of others.

Marlene had recently retired from her full time job and now volunteered as a pink lady at the hospital, where she worked in the gift shop. The people she met were often there visiting loved ones who would never leave the premises, and Marlene found within herself a deep well of compassion, along with a propensity for offering meaningful words of comfort. Perhaps that came from her own first hand experience dealing with the death of her mother. She understood how useless all of the usual platitudes were to those who were grieving. They didn't need banality; what they craved were ears that hear, and hearts that understand. She was also very good at listening and empathizing.

She now laid a hand on Jimmy's knee. "I know how hard that's going to be for you."

Jimmy affected a wry smile. "Pretty bad when your own mother doesn't know who you are."

"But you understand it has nothing to do with you, or how much she loves you. It's just the disease."

"Yeah, I know, but it still hurts."

"Well, let's just see how things go; it may not be as bad as we anticipate."

Jimmy scoffed. "That's not what my sisters tell me. Like you said, nothing's changed since last time, except that it's more so."

Marlene could see that any words she might use to cheer him would be inadequate, so she simply took his hand in hers and smiled at him hopefully. The flight was a relatively long one, and took place at an hour usually dedicated to sleep, so the two of them gradually succumbed to the impulse.

Jimmy had always been an inquisitive, observant child. As a toddler he was very tactile, and had, on occasion, been found squishing his mother's hand cream through his fingers, or spreading himself with butter. Nadine's knitting needles, because of their peculiar shape and feel, were always an attraction. It was, however, unfailingly necessary for him to unravel her current project in order to fully experience their uniqueness.

When he was about three years old he took one of Nadine's clocks apart to see what made it tick–literally. Of course, he didn't possess the skills required to put it back together again, which elicited a few harsh words from his mother. But, from that time forward, it seemed he was always exploring, investigating, or tinkering with something, and forever inquiring.

Case in point: as a small child, while observing his mother scrubbing the floor, he couldn't keep his hands out of her mop bucket. When she told him he needed to stay out of the water, he asked, "Why?"

"Because it's dirty," Nadine explained.

"Why is it dirty?"

"Because the dirt comes off the floor, onto the sponge, and into the water."

"Why is the floor dirty?"

"Because people walk on it with dirty shoes."

"Why are their shoes dirty?"

"Because they've been walking in the dirt."

"Why?"

He'd never been particularly keen on sports, preferring the more analytical pursuits. That is, once he outgrew his cowboy obsession, which began on his second Christmas when Santa delivered a hobby horse and a Hop-Along Cassidy suit. For weeks he refused to remove his hat when he went to bed at night, and it wasn't long before he was riding that plastic pony so violently that it actually moved across the floor.

He was probably Hop-Along until he was three and a half, when he became Bart Maverick. The family had recently moved into a new home, and he proclaimed to the neighborhood children that he was none other than that famous and well-loved TV character. The bloody noses and black eyes that resulted did not deter him in the slightest; each day he would join his new playmates, inform them once again of his identity, and return home battered and bruised.

After the family had lived there about a month, Melvin and Nadine attended a pot luck dinner at their church. When they introduced themselves to their table mates and explained a little of their background and family dynamics, the woman next to Nadine suddenly jolted to life. "That's *your* little boy! I'm his Sunday school teacher and I've been trying ever since you moved in to find out what his name is. All he would tell me was, "Bart Maverick."

Jimmy's school career began normally; his grades were good, and he seemed to be adjusting and participating well. Then, gradually, his functioning began to decline. Nadine assumed that it was merely the increased difficulty of his school work, which he could no longer seem to manage.

Considering his substandard performance in high school, there didn't seem much point in pursuing a college degree, so Jimmy went to work as an auto mechanic. Then, tiring of the constant grease under his fingernails, he'd tried construction: sheet rocking, and subsequently painting. It was after he got fed up with low wages, lack of work, and labor unions, that he decided to further his education.

It all began with the advent of the home computer. Jimmy's interest was sparked. He began bringing home books from the library, and studying the intricacies of electronics. His first project was to construct his own processing system; then encouraged by his success, he designed and built a small robot, which he could control from the computer keyboard. Unfortunately for Nadine, however, the little mechanical man wasn't programmed to do windows or dishes.

Finally, his appetite whetted, Jimmy enrolled in the local technical college. With his quick mind and insatiable desire for knowledge, he was soon instructing the professors—a practice which did not endear him to those supposedly learned men. Even though the earning of an associate's degree was the extent of his formal education, he proved to be something of a genius in his field and became invaluable to every company for which he worked. And, whenever one of his sisters needed technical advice, it was always, "Call Jimmy. He'll know what to do."

Abigail, Tracey, and their husbands all appeared at the airport to welcome Jimmy and Marlene off the plane. Then Barry and Abigail showed them to the car and the four of them headed for the red brick dwelling the Bartletts called home. Once away from the airport Abigail turned to face the occupants of the back seat. "I got a call from Mom's nurse this morning. She wants me to arrange a party for Mom tomorrow night." She pursed her lips. "Personally, I think it's a foolish idea. Mom'd just as soon spit in our eye, literally, as to have us all in her room, partying."

Jimmy frowned his disappointment. "So she's gotten mean?"

"Oh, Jimmy, I know it's hard, but it's nothing personal. She's just mad at the world, and since she doesn't usually recognize any of her family, we're simply lumped together with the rest of humanity. She, once in awhile, seems to like Tracey okay, but It doesn't matter what I do, she's continually infuriated with me. Who can say what demons posses her mind? Don't be offended if she gets ornery with you."

"How do you deal with that?"

Abigail shrugged. "Not very well, I'm afraid. Tracey and I should soon become immune to her venom, since we get bitten on a regular basis." She immediately regretted her choice of words. "I'm sorry, Jimmy. That was a stupid thing to say. Sometimes the frustration just gets the better of me."

Jimmy gazed out the side window, attempting to hide his raw emotions, but couldn't suppress the tears in his voice. "Isn't she ever lucid?"

Abigail sighed wearily. "Not that I've seen; not in the last couple of years. That's why I think a so-called party is a waste of time. But, much against my better judgment, I promised Lisa I'd make it happen. She wouldn't take no for an answer, so prepare yourself for a few hours of verbal abuse. Also, we'd better get naps in beforehand; Lisa doesn't come on duty until eleven, so it'll be a late night."

They arrived home, and Abigail settled her guests in the spare bedroom. It was late, so after wrapping the last of her gifts, she crawled in next to her already slumbering husband and strived for peaceful oblivion. But sleep wouldn't come. The anticipation of a Christmas celebration with her mother filled her with dread. It was bad enough that she and Tracey had to endure Nadine's onslaughts, she hated to subject Jimmy to the feelings of rejection and abandonment that would inevitably result.

As she considered the Christmases of her youth and the festive holiday atmosphere that permeated their home, even in the lean years, she was filled with longing for a return to those happy times. In the solitude assured by Barry's deep, even breathing, she allowed the tears to fall unrestrained onto the pillow, and again asked herself, "What is the reason for it all? Why should anyone have to be put through this?"

It was a moot question. In the deepest regions of her mind and heart she knew the answer. Suffering was a part of the human existence and served a divine purpose. She just wished she understood better what that purpose was. The orthodox explanation readily came to mind: to make us strong, to teach us certain valuable lessons. But had she learned anything from the adversity in her life? Was she, indeed, any stronger for the afflictions she'd endured?

She supposed that, compared to Tracey, her own life seemed pretty uneventful. But there had been some rough times, occasions about which she'd kept silent. No reason to worry her family; none of them had been in a position to help.

Shortly after she and Barry were married, he had lost his job. Abigail was just beginning her career and was unable to support them both on what she, alone, was making. He'd become depressed; she'd become frustrated. The bills were not getting paid. Their utilities were being turned off. They were fighting, constantly: he rationalizing his inability to find work; she claiming that she'd married a loser. And, all the while, pretending to her family that everything was peachy.

Then, feeling emasculated by Abigail's constant onslaughts and demoralized by his own feelings of guilt, Barry began to drink. That's when Abigail was slammed harshly against the jagged rocks of reality, and finally admitted to herself that she needed help. Their sporadic church activity notwithstanding, she called her bishop and blurted out the whole story. Consequently returning to full fellowship, they received counseling, job leads, and financial assistance until they were again on their feet. She had to hand it to Barry; he'd pulled himself back from the abyss, and from that moment on, had kept his feet on terra firma. They'd managed to stay afloat through succeeding waves of turbulence, and that furtive segment of their lives remained a silent memory.

Then, when Abigail became pregnant with her first child, she practically shouted it from the rooftops. Her friends and family were informed of her condition on the day of her first visit to the doctor, after he confirmed her suspicions. She stopped at J.C. Penney on the way home from her appointment and purchased diapers and gowns, little booties and burp cloths. Barry passed out bubble gum cigars to all of his friends at work the following day. They rode on a pink cloud for the next ten weeks. And then the storm broke; Abigail began to hemorrhage. There was no saving the baby. All of the hope, all of the anticipation, all of the excitement were buried with that tiny bundle.

Yes, Abigail had had some rough times, but for all of her trials, she still didn't feel any more honorable or wise. With a heavy sigh she swung her feet to the floor and trudged to the kitchen for something to help her sleep: a Tylenol PM? No, she'd then be muzzy-headed for a full twelve hours. Maybe some warm milk with sugar—what her mom used to call "Mormon tea"—would be enough to gag her noisy thoughts. She pulled the nearly empty milk carton from the refrigerator, realizing that she'd forgotten to put in sufficient stores for Jimmy's breakfast needs. "Well, he'll just have to settle for hot chocolate," she said aloud.

"Who will?" came a voice from behind her.

Turning, she beheld her brother standing in the doorway. She held up the bottle in her hand and shrugged. "Sorry, but I'm about to diminish your supply by one cup."

"That's all the milk you've got?" he reproved, as he took a seat at the counter. "You're slipping, Sis!"

Abigail's expression was bemused as she pulled a mug from the cupboard and filled it. "A couple of days ago that comment would have sounded to me like a dire prognostication."

"I didn't mean anything sinister by it."

"I know. It's just that, for awhile there, with some of the things that were going on with Mom, I'd begun to question the state of my own mental health." She placed her cup of milk into the microwave and pushed the necessary buttons. Then, leaning on the counter across from her brother, she recounted the incident with Lisa, the aftermath of which had produced in her the fear that she was soon destined for the same fate as their mother. Jimmy interjected words of acknowledgment, empathy, and surprise, as indicated. "You know," she concluded. "Alzheimer's sometimes strikes people at my age."

Jimmy chuckled. "Well, if I notice any further symptoms, I'll be the first to tell you."

Abigail snorted. "That's what Tracey said!"

Jimmy turned his palms up. "That's what brothers and sisters are for, isn't it?" he joked. "So, tell me more about this nurse."

"It's really uncanny how much she resembles our Meese, not only in size and coloring, but also facial features. It was like a slam in the chest the first time I saw her."

"Ironic that she'd be assigned to Mom."

The microwave beeped and Abigail retrieved the steaming cup, then stirred sugar into it and took a tentative sip. "I just wish I knew what to make of her. She seems nice enough, but the whole thing is so disturbing. I'm afraid that Tracey and I weren't exactly cordial to her. This thing about Mom and her talking, I don't know how that can possibly be true. And yet, why would she lie?"

"Did she mention anything, in particular, that might have triggered these fleeting episodes of sanity?"

Abigail shook her head. "No, and she's the only one who has ever witnessed them."

Jimmy pondered for a moment. "Maybe it's simply her appearance, the fact that she looks so much like Meese, that briefly pulls Mom back from her personal abyss."

"But, why her, and not Tracey or me? Well, not me anyway. Like I said, she sometimes responds to Tracey, but never to me."

Jimmy considered his response. "Well, Meese is a part of the past, where Mom's mind is evidently stuck, when it functions at all. You and Tracey are in the here and now. You two have matured with the intervening years." He laughed. "At least *you* have. Tracey, on the other hand–." He shrugged and Abigail chuckled in agreement. "You're not the same pimply-faced youth she envisions in her imagination."

Abigail punched him on the shoulder. "Thanks for reminding me of my less than creamy adolescent complexion!"

"Well, look on the bright side: to Mom, you'll always be young."

"And pimply-faced!"

Jimmy shrugged. "You gotta take the bad with the good; nobody can have it all."

Abigail circled the counter and wrapped her arms around her brother. "Oh, Jimmy, I'm so glad you're here. I've missed you terribly."

"Yeah, too bad we live so far away. Even though I'm relieved that I don't have to deal with Mom's illness, I feel like a slug, leaving you and Trace to shoulder all the responsibility by yourselves."

"Well, you're here now, Bro, and I can't tell you how glad I am."

It was time for the shift change at the center, and Nadine was looking forward to another pleasant night of reminiscing. She had, by now, quit fretting over the possible termination of Lisa's nightly visits. She knew, with certainty, that her little confidant would not disappoint her. The two of them were inexorably connected.

As Lisa entered the room, Nadine opened her arms, inviting an embrace. "Is it all right if I call you 'Meese,'" she asked, "when we're here alone?"

"Of course," Lisa smiled. "I'd like that." She sat at Nadine's side and took her hand. "So, what tales have you to tell me tonight?"

Nadine chuckled. "You are balm to a mother's soul. Talking about the past makes me realize how blessed I've been. In spite of all of my failings, my children are caring, industrious, honorable men and women. I wouldn't trade them for anything–or anyone–in the world." Her eyes filled and she blinked to halt the tears.

Then, taking a deep breath, she began, "Right around the time that Danny was born, my older children started leaving home. Jimmy had earned his associate degree, and then gone to work for a computer company. So, just shortly before Danny arrived, Jimmy moved into an apartment closer to his job. Abby was going to school out of state, and living on campus, so was only home in the summer time, and even then she worked, so wasn't around much. And, of course, Meese left us right around then. Tracey was kind of in and out, as her circumstances changed.

"We lived in Rigby until Danny was about eleven, and then Melvin was transferred back to Utah, so we left the land of perpetual wind storms and moved to the land of perpetual road construction; we've lived here ever since. Of course, in the middle of our move, when Melvin went back to get another load of furniture, the truck broke down–big surprise. So, at ten-thirty at night, I hauled Danny out of bed and drove to Pocatello to pick up my stranded husband. I believe that was the last time for that kind of emergency. Melvin started making better money, and from then on, we were able to buy more dependable vehicles.

"Tracey was married to Dale by this time, so it was just the three of us. About a year after the move I went to Boise to spend a week with Tracey, helping her out. She was pregnant and had developed toxemia, so was ordered to stay in bed. She and her husband were living in a trailer house at this time and had it fixed up really cute. I was very impressed with Dale while I was there–he took such good care of Tracey, and was so thoughtful with her. After all of her earlier fiascos I was glad to see that she had finally found a good man.

"Earlier fiascos?"

"Suffice it to say that, up until that point, her life had not been a bed of roses. So, it was nice to see her getting along so well, except, of course, for the toxemia. After I left, some women from church came in to help for another week, and then Abby took a week off work to stay with her.

"Tracey's infection eventually cleared up, but the doctor then could hear no fetal heartbeat. He induced labor and Tracey delivered a stillborn daughter, Britt Loren. We, of course, drove to Boise for the graveside services."

"You've had your share of tragedy, haven't you," Lisa commiserated.

"Yes, I have, and for a lot of years I felt pretty sorry for myself."

"But you survived and are a better person for it."

"Am I?" Nadine asked, her own questions mirroring those of her oldest daughter. "Sometimes I wonder."

"It's often hard to see improvement in ourselves, because it usually comes about so gradually. It's easy to believe that we've always been as we are now. But, in truth, Heavenly Father is the only one who never changes, is the same yesterday, today, and forever. You, on the other hand–"

Nadine grimaced. "I suppose you're right, although, to myself, I don't seem any different now than I was sixty years ago. Well," she guffawed, "except for the sagging, decrepit body."

"Which you'll soon shed."

"Yes! Won't that be a relief, to be young again?"

"Well," Lisa mused, "that's hard for me to say, since I've never been old."

Nadine nodded. "As they say, 'it's not for sissies.' Anyway, soon after Tracey delivered her stillborn baby, Jimmy met Marlene, who then became his wife, and eventually, all of my children blazed their trail to Utah, with a couple of detours along the way. Well, actually, Abby and Barry were living here before Melvin and Danny and I made the move.

"We then began holding official family reunions. Over Memorial Day weekend, that first year, we camped out in the middle of a field close to Strawberry Reservoir. Abby and Barry had a tent trailer, Melvin and I had a small camper, and the rest of the family slept in tents. Although Abby and Tracey were both very pregnant, they were good sports about the rugged adventure. It rained the whole time we were there and we were all miserable, but my burgeoning girls probably suffered the most.

They stuck it out, though. Now all of their children are grown and married and having babies of their own.

"A later reunion was held at Bear Lake, and because we wanted to make sure we got a camping spot, Jimmy and Marlene and I went up early in the day and secured a place. The rest of the family were coming up together after work, and bringing Melvin with them. The campground was pretty full and the only spot we could find was a little way off the beaten path, so I took paper sacks and marked them with instructions such as 'Keep going,' or 'You're not there yet,' and posted them along the road. Always needing to have my little joke, I didn't add my name or any other identifying mark to the signs. It was a test to see how well my family knew me; I thought that Tracey and Abby would probably recognize my particular brand of humor.

"When all of them finally arrived, Tracey told me that, on the way, Melvin kept saying, 'Your mom didn't write those.' But Tracey and Abby just kept on insisting, 'Yes, she did,' and continued following the paper signs. They said, 'We *knew* that was you!'" Nadine chuckled. "I was pretty certain my girls were smart enough to figure it out.

"Oh!" she blurted. "Another fun memory just popped into my head. When Danny was about ten, a lake was constructed on the other side of Rigby. Melvin was able to lay his hands on a boat–it was repossessed, so very cheap–and Danny and I learned to water ski.

"A new family, the Shaffers, had just moved into the neighborhood, and I asked the mom one day if she dared go water skiing with someone who had never launched or driven a boat. Kathy was game, even though it'd been years since she'd handled any type of water craft (she was originally from Florida, so had done some water skiing when she was younger). That afternoon we hooked up the trailer, loaded the kids (she had five) into the back of the pickup and took off for Rigby Lake.

"I managed to figure out the controls, and everything went fine until a thunder storm came up and it started pouring rain. Kathy was up on the skis, and after dropping into the water, couldn't pull herself back into the boat. We hauled in the skis while she swam over to an anchored raft in the middle of the lake; she couldn't get up on that either. So I headed the boat in her direction to pick her up, and when I got close to the raft I put the engine in neutral. The wind was blowing so hard that it blew the boat head on into the raft and almost ran it over the top of poor Kathy. I shifted into reverse, but the ski rope was still in the water and got tangled around the prop, which killed the engine, so I lifted up the motor while Kathy untangled it. Meanwhile, the middle of the rope got hooked onto something underneath the raft, so Kathy dove down to undo that. I then got the engine started again, finally got Kathy into the boat, and headed back to the dock. By that time the storm had subsided, but we were all freezing, so the outing was abandoned."

"And that's a *fun* memory?" marveled Lisa.

"Well, it all turned out okay, and it's fun because it was the beginning of our daily jaunts to the lake. Kathy and I pooled the contents of our piggy banks each day to buy gasoline (it probably cost about twenty cents a gallon), and she and I took turns driving and skiing. It was a great summer!"

Lisa nodded. "For sure."

"Back now to our move to Utah; after we'd been there for a couple of years, we decided to build a dome home. I'd seen one in Idaho and fallen in love with the uniqueness of it. Construction began in March and was supposed to be completed in forty-five days. Finally, after eight long, frustrating months we moved in, on Thanksgiving Day (shades of the past). We'd already invited the whole family for dinner, thinking that we would be all settled long before this time, but a few things were still unfinished." Nadine chuckled. "The story of our lives, huh? At least, this time we had a toilet! Just no floor coverings. So the carpet layers came and worked around our ankles while we enjoyed the feast–we didn't invite them to join us, by the way. Fortunately, they finished before we did and were able to go home to their own dinners.

"I think I loved that house more than the one we built in Salem. Again, I thought we'd be there for the rest of our lives. Of course, I thought that about every house we ever lived in. The master bedroom was on the main floor, so I figured, when I got old and feeble, I'd only need to climb the stairs about once a month to clean." She grinned. "I wasn't exactly an obsessive housekeeper. I never had been a daily duster, and found that failing eyesight was, in some ways, a real blessing. I remember my aging aunt telling me once that, because she and her husband couldn't see well anymore, they still looked good to one another."

Lisa laughed. "You see, there's always a bright side."

Nadine nodded. "That's one thing I *have* learned: more often than not, what seems to be a tragedy turns out to be a blessing. I remember once when, against my own desires, I was released from a fairly prestigious position at church. I think I cried for a week. I *know* I cried for a week! They gave me no explanation, so of course I assumed that I had not been measuring up. That was a real blow to my pride.

"Then they asked me to teach an adult Sunday school class, and I cried for another week. I was no scriptorian! A few days later I was belly-achin' to one of the bishop's counselors, who happened to be a good friend, and he informed me that they had been trying for six months to make this change, but the higher-ups had refused, because they didn't want to release me from my other calling. As it turned out, teaching the scriptures to grownups was one of the most rewarding things I've ever done."

"All those wasted tears," chided Lisa.

"If I'd collected all the tears, wasted and otherwise, that I've shed over my lifetime, they'd have had no need to pipe in water for Rigby Lake," she stated wryly. "But where was I?"

"Teaching Sunday school."

"Yes. I believe that was just before Danny turned sixteen. I remember that the next spring, to aid me in my lesson preparations, we used our income tax return to buy a computer–the first one we ever owned. With the remaining funds we purchased a motorcycle, the intention being that Danny would use it for transportation to and from school. Well, I decided that, if we were going to own a motorcycle, I was going to ride it. So I learned–after a fashion–and Danny and I both went at the same time to get our operator's licenses. Danny was very comfortable on the bike and easily passed his road test. I, on the other hand, knocked over every other cone along the course. The officer was very kind and passed me anyway, with the express stipulation that I 'stay off any busy roads!'

"Abby's husband Barry was incredulous when I told him I had my license–incredulous and a little miffed–since he had failed his first attempt at acquiring the same. I have to tell you, I was pretty proud of myself for being an almost sixty-year-old with a motorcycle license. Even after we got rid of the bike, I kept renewing my license just so I could say I had one. Of course, eventually, common sense overruled foolish pride."

"Good for you."

"Well, I'm sure there were other instances when pride won out over wisdom. Anyway, in all the time that we had that motorcycle, Danny took only one bad spill, when he went riding up into the nearby hills. He drove the bike back home afterward, but wouldn't let me see the damage done to his leg, just ordered me to take him to the hospital for stitches. I, however, had the last laugh. When they were cleaning and sewing up the wound, I had a clear view of the whole grisly mess."

"And it didn't bother you?"

"I always thought I should have been a doctor or a nurse. Once, when Jimmy was about ten or twelve, he was playing at an old shack he and his friends used as their 'hut' in the yard behind us. He was standing on top of it when the roof caved in. As he plummeted downward, his arms went up over his head and a spike that was protruding from an inside wall caught him in the biceps and ripped his arm open.

"His dad and I were in our backyard, working on some landscaping, when suddenly Melvin stopped in his tracks and said to me, "I wonder what Jimmy is up to." He scaled the back fence and arrived at the shed just as Jimmy fell, so was able to lift him off of the nail.

"We ran him to the hospital, where the doctor stitched him up. I was quite fascinated by the whole process and watched as he mended several layers of tissue. Melvin, on the other hand, had to escape to the waiting room to keep from fainting.

"Fortunately, the nerves and muscles were undamaged and Jimmy recovered without any lasting disability. He told me later that the worst part of the whole ordeal was explaining to his friends what he considered to be a stupid accident.

"Neither of my sons ever wanted anyone to be aware of their injuries. Maybe they thought it diminished them in some way. When Danny was just little, he somehow got a black eye, and hid under an afghan all day for fear that someone would see it. Then, when he was

146

a little older and broke his arm, he scooted under the kitchen table whenever anyone came over.

"My boys also never touted their accomplishments or acts of heroism. When Danny was in his teens, he went on a river trip with the young people from church. If he hadn't gone, two of the girls in the group wouldn't be around today. He saved them both from drowning after their raft capsized, by pulling them out of the water, one in each hand, and lifting them onto his own raft; thank goodness for all of his body-building. Of course, Danny never told me what had happened. I found out about it when the girls' parents later expressed their deep gratitude to me.

"That was the same year I was asked to participate in a production of 'The Sound of Music.' The director needed someone who could reach high C, and I was recruited. I was cast as one of the nuns, who sang all of their songs a capella, with only a bell to sound the beginning pitch. Unfortunately, the woman who took it upon herself to get us started on each of the numbers was slightly tone deaf (at least as far as the bell was concerned), and unfailingly pitched us two or three steps higher than was accurate. Consequently, after I joined the cast, the other sopranos all dropped down to the second part, leaving me as the only one carrying the higher notes. I'll tell you, some of them were so far up there, I nearly fainted from lack of oxygen."

Nadine chortled ruefully. "On closing night, during the finale, when I made the climb to that formidable high C, my voice cracked."

"How embarrassing!" Lisa sympathized.

"Oh, that's putting it mildly. I wanted to perish on the spot. But, I lived to sing another day, in other productions, although I was never again called upon to perform a high C, thank goodness.

"There were other humiliating incidents. Once, when I was singing with a trio, we did a program for the local gathering of the Republican Party. I had on a pair of new panty hose, which didn't want to stay where they belonged. Since our program lasted about forty-five minutes with no breaks and a good deal of action, by the time we were through, the top of my hose was down around my knees."

"What did you do?"

"What *could* I do? It wasn't like I could just reach down and pull them up. So, after I took my bow, I turned around and hobbled off, knock-kneed, to the restroom."

Nadine sighed deeply. "I spent my whole life singing, until in my seventies, when my voice started to go. One of the hardest things about getting old was surrendering the attributes that had always identified my individuality. Suddenly I began to wonder, 'Who the heck am I, and what purpose do I have for living?'

"Years ago my best friend had to put her husband into a facility like this one. She was feeling so guilty because he was forced to relinquish his autonomy, but I told her, 'We all, eventually, bit by bit, have to give up the things that have always been important to us.' When you're young, you think it will never happen; you'll never be old. And the next morning you wake up and find out you're sixty. So, I say, 'Enjoy what you have while you have it. It'll only last about thirty minutes.'"

CHAPTER 11 - *Friday & Saturday, December 24ᵗʰ & 25ᵗʰ*

Abigail stood with her family in front of Nadine's closed door, their arms loaded with goodies for the midnight feast. She took a deep breath. "Well, here goes nothing. Don't say I didn't warn you."

Jimmy laid his arm across her shoulders. "It's okay, Sis. It's not your job to protect us, you know. We're able to take our own lumps. So, let's just make the best of it."

Barry pushed open the heavy door and stood aside while the others entered. Nadine was sitting up in bed, a cryptic expression on her face, as Lisa arose from her seat and turned toward the family, offering each a smile and a warm hello as they gathered. Melvin was immediately settled in a bedside chair, while the sisters busied themselves arranging the table brought in for the occasion. Abigail hardly dared look at her mother, fearing that eye contact might trigger the usual barrage.

The others gave Nadine the obligatory greeting and kiss on the cheek, to which she responded with a slight fluttering of the eyelids, but otherwise passively, and Abigail counted it as a blessing that her mother's mouth, so far, was silent.

Finally Abigail turned, a tentative curve to her lips, and gave Nadine a kiss on the forehead. "How are you doing tonight, Mom?"

Nadine flashed the smile of bygone days and answered, "I couldn't be better, now that you're all here."

Abigail jerked to attention, completely flummoxed; Melvin smiled and patted his wife's arm; Tracey's eyes widened in surprise; Jimmy laughed delightedly; Marlene sighed with relief; the two husbands looked at each other in amazement. Nadine continued as if nothing were out of the ordinary, "Jimmy, I'm so glad that you and Marlene could come this year. I've missed you terribly."

Jimmy gave Abigail a mildly accusatory look–to which she responded with an expression of befuddlement–then he walked to his mother's side and grasped her hands. "I'm glad, too, Mom, and happy that you're feeling so well tonight."

Nadine surveyed the group around her, then turned her head toward Lisa. "I always feel well when Lisa's here; we have some good talks. Well, actually, she doesn't do much talking, just a lot of listening. It was her idea to have a party, though." She chuckled mischievously. "We can't get too wild, now; if we disturb the other residents, the staff will make you leave."

Tracey was all smiles as she beheld her mother's metamorphosis, but Abigail couldn't staunch her tears. "Abby," Nadine gently scolded, "you shouldn't be crying; this is a happy occasion."

"That's why I'm crying, Mom, because I'm so happy."

Nadine opened her arms and folded them around her oldest daughter. "I know, Sweetie. I'm just teasing you. I feel like crying, myself."

"Well," interjected Tracey, "I think, before this gets any more maudlin, we'd better start the party. Who's going to bless the food? Dad? You want to call on someone?"

Melvin nodded. "I'll do it, myself." He then offered thanks for Nadine's sudden return to them, for the lives of all of his children, the love they shared, and the fact that they were together tonight. Finally he asked that the food be blessed to their benefit, then closed his prayer."

"Okay," enthused Tracey, "everyone grab some grub and pull up a chair. Mom, you're the guest of honor; what would you like?"

"I can get her a plate," offered Lisa. "You all just serve yourselves."

Jimmy leaned over to Abigail and whispered, "You were right about Mom's nurse; she's the spit 'n' image of Meese."

Abigail nodded. "Unsettling, isn't it?"

"Have you mentioned it to her?"

"Um-hm. She says she must have one of those faces, and that everyone has a twin somewhere. You know, the usual garbage. When I was in college I was always being mistaken for one person or another and told that I 'look just like' so-and-so, but I never looked *this* much like anyone. I've never seen such a resemblance before."

"Spooky," he agreed.

When everyone was seated with a plate on their laps, Jimmy remarked, "All this food reminds me of the backyard barbeques we used to have. You remember that time when Tracey ate too many black olives and immediately threw up all over the table?"

There was a general burst of laughter, along with a few groans, and Tracey retaliated with, "Yeah, well, at least I didn't go wading in the canal in Dad's brand new leather work boots."

Jimmy almost choked. "I didn't do that!"

Abigail hooted. "Ha! That's what you tried to tell Dad when you sloshed into the house with the incriminating evidence right there on your own two feet!"

151

"Oh?" Jimmy sneered playfully. "Well, you weren't so perfect, yourself, little sis. I remember when you lost Mom's favorite earrings and then blamed Meese for it."

"She was always blaming one of us for all the naughty things she did!" accused Tracey.

"I was never naughty," objected Abigail. "Innocent mistakes, that's all they ever were."

Nadine listened in delicious contentment as the teasing recriminations flew back and forth, complete with feigned indignation and a good deal of laughter.

At the first lull in the conversation Lisa looked at her watch, then announced, "I have a surprise for all of you."

"Is this the one you were telling me about?" asked Nadine, her eyes sparkling.

Lisa merely shrugged noncommittally. "I have to leave for a few minutes, but you're going to like what I bring back with me." All eyes followed as she exited the room.

"I wonder if she's got Santa waiting out in the hall," suggested Tracey.

"You going to sit on his lap?" Jimmy teased.

"You better believe it! My Christmas list is in my pocket."

"I know what I'll say to him," remarked Abigail. "I'll tell him he'd better have one of those new IPads on his sleigh."

Barry gasped. "Is *that* what you wanted?"

Abigail gave her husband a sidelong glance, then turned to Tracey. "I hope your guest room is ready, because Barry may be moving in sometime tomorrow."

The door swished open then and Lisa reappeared, followed by a young man in battle fatigues. Nadine's eyes glued themselves to his face, as deep furrows creased her brow. He proceeded slowly to her side as sudden intakes of breath were heard from the onlookers. Nadine's jaw dropped slightly, while Melvin and the others sat in stunned silence. "Danny?" she murmured. "Is that you?"

The young man took her hands and smiled. "It's me, Mom."

There was a disbelieving chorus of "Danny?" as the room's occupants recovered from their shock. Food was forgotten, along with all former bantering, as the siblings stood and gathered around their long lost brother. He lingeringly hugged them each in turn before the questions began. "But, what happened to you?" "Where have you been?" "Why didn't anyone let us know they'd found you?" "How–?" When–?" Who–?"

"I'm sorry you were all given so much worry, but there was no way for me to get in touch. To begin with, I was captured by the al-Queda and held prisoner for a couple of years." At these words there were gasps of horror from his family, which he let go unheeded. "Since then I've been on special assignment. That's about all I can say. You know how those things are: very hush hush."

Nadine's fingers had flown to her mouth. "You were captured? Oh, Danny."

He took her hand in his. "It's in the past, Mom, and I'd just as soon we leave it there."

She studied each plane of her son's beloved face, her eyes glistening. "I never gave up hope, you know. I prayed every day that you'd return home."

Danny looked at his mother with tenderness. "Well, Mom, your prayers were answered." He looked at the members of his family, his eyes lingering momentarily on each countenance, then lifted a knee and perched sidesaddle on the edge of Nadine's bed. He smiled in an effort to lighten the mood. "What a great reunion!"

"But where did you come from?" Abigail wasn't satisfied with his evasive excuses. "How do you happen to be here?"

Danny waved a hand in the nurse's direction. "It was all Lisa's doing. She and I go back a ways; we've worked together in the past."

Abigail turned to Lisa. "You were in the service?" Her tone was incredulous, but Lisa merely smiled. "That doesn't seem possible; you're so young!"

"A youthful appearance can be a valuable asset in certain situations," remarked Lisa.

"She's also well connected," Danny declared, "and knew what strings to pull. So here I am." All eyes turned again to Lisa, their astonishment clearly apparent, and their most salient question needing no auditory delivery.

Lisa shrugged. "It pays to be on good terms with the right people."

The inquisition resumed at full force, with Danny doing his best to dodge any questions that required security-breaching answers. Finally he called the whole thing to a halt, gesturing toward the empty chairs. "Go ahead and get back to your meals. The important thing is that we're all here." His siblings, however, were reluctant to return to their abandoned repasts, and Tracey couldn't resist giving her little brother an additional hug. Despite the difference in their ages, they had always maintained a sweet bond between them. "You, too, Danny. Have some food."

He waved a hand in refusal. "Maybe later." She gave him one last pat on the shoulder and returned to her seat. Danny's smile was ecstatic as he gazed at the lot of them. "It's so good to see you all. You'll never know how much I've missed you." He took a deep breath and huffed it out. "Well." He slapped his knee. "It sounded like you were having a good time before I came in. What was all the chatter about?"

Abigail chuckled. "The usual, whenever we get together. We were dredging up all our old grievances to rehash them."

"It's vital, you know, that we do that," interjected Tracey. "We wouldn't want to forgive and forget!"

"No danger of that," Jimmy chortled. "You'll always be there to remind us."

"Yeah, well, as I recall," countered Tracey, "you were the one who started it this time."

"You know what Mom always said, 'It takes two to tango,' or sometimes three or four."

Nadine laughed to hear her own words reiterated. Many were the times when she'd used that very counsel as one or the other of her children claimed innocence of first offense. She was enjoying this enormously!

"Since I missed all those years while you were growing up, and haven't heard any of your scathing recitals for such a long time, go for it," Danny implored.

Abigail grunted and rolled her eyes. "Where to begin?"

"How about the time," Tracey recalled, "that Jimmy wired our old tricycle to the electric fence and then told the little neighbor boy he could have the trike if he'd come and ride it home?" While the others clucked their feigned disapproval, Jimmy merely grinned his admitted guilt.

"The worst was when he called Mom a liar," chided Abigail. "That's the only time I've ever heard a bad word cross the lips of our straight-laced little mother."

"And you ran to the phone and called Dad at work to tell on her," Tracey hooted.

"He didn't get it, though. I kept telling him that Mom had called Jimmy a 'smart A,' but he thought I meant smart Alec and couldn't figure out why it was such a big deal."

Nadine jumped in at that point. "Honesty was the one thing on which I prided myself; I wasn't about to let a little 'smart A,'" she grinned at Jimmy, "attack my only virtue."

"And then there was the time that Jimmy caught himself on fire," added Abigail.

Jimmy grimaced. "I was burning the trash for Dad. I knew he always poured on gasoline to start the fire, so I merely followed suit. But then, after I lighted it, I noticed the gas can was too close, so I kicked it out of the way. How was I supposed to know that it would splash all over me?"

"When it happened," Nadine interjected, "I was at the church, rehearsing with the women's chorus, and got a phone call from the neighbors across the way. Scared me to death. The problem was, by the time I got home, they had already treated his burns. Because they believed in herbal medicine and natural healing, they'd smeared his whole chest with honey. When we got to the emergency room, the doctor was, of course, appalled, but I have to admit Jimmy healed without any scars."

"I have a memory about Jimmy," chimed in Danny. "When I was just little, he told me that the way to catch a bird was to put salt on its tail. Do you know how many hours I spent out in the back yard with the salt shaker?" This was one account they hadn't heard before, and there was an immediate explosion of laughter.

"Why is everyone picking on me?" Jimmy grumbled good-naturedly.

"Because you're the one who was always up to no good!" declared Abigail.

"That's for sure," chided Tracey. "I remember when you tied the handlebars of my bicycle to the poles on the swing set so I could 'practice balancing.' You knew very well that, as soon as I climbed on, I'd take a face plant."

Jimmy arranged his face into an almost believable manifestation of ingenuous ignorance. "What do you mean? How could I have known that?"

"Because you knew all about everything scientific, electronic, or dynamic."

"Jimmy was always the inquisitive one," Nadine affirmed. "I remember once when he asked me why cowboys never had to go to the bathroom. I assured him that they did, indeed, and asked what made him think otherwise. 'Because,' he said, 'they never show it on television.'"

"Those were the good old days," smirked Abigail. "Today, he wouldn't have to ask."

"You're right about that," agreed Nadine. "As they used to say, 'We've come a long way, Baby.' Anyway, it was about that same time that Jimmy wanted to know why our neighbor smoked. I told him that it was for the same reason that people eat candy, even though they know it isn't good for them. They get into the habit and can't quit. I then explained, at great length, the meaning of habit—that some were good and some were bad, and that we should have good habits, but avoid the other kind. When I finished, about twenty minutes later, I asked, 'Now, Jimmy, do you understand why Mr. Harrison smokes?'

"'Yes,' he answered, and I felt so proud of myself for making it clear to him. Then he explained, 'Because it tastes like candy.'"

They laughed at the well known and long forgotten stories, but Tracey was still contemplating her bicycle experience. She turned again to Jimmy. "You'll be happy to know that you weren't the only fly in my face cream when it came to bike riding. After I finally did learn how (no thanks to my kind big brother), there was one weekend when we were staying with the Davises, down in Ogden. The twins wanted to go for a ride, so generously loaned me one of their bikes. Just as we were starting down a steep hill that crossed a busy intersection, one of them hollered, 'Oh, by the way, you've got no brakes.'"

"Let's face it," countered Jimmy, "you never did have the brain power to operate a moving vehicle. Remember when you went three-wheeling with your friend's family, and wrecked their machine?"

Tracey was accustomed to her brother's slurs about her mental capabilities, but pretended to take exception. "Everyone knows how dangerous those things are. People were always getting hurt on them."

"I have to say," Nadine interrupted, "you did seem to have your share of accidents. The hospital called me when that one happened, to let me know that you'd been hurt and they were treating you. The next time I got that kind of call, it was from the police. That was when you and your friends hitched a ride with some boys in a pickup. You all piled into the back end, and then the driver rolled the truck. It's a wonder you weren't killed, and that I, myself, didn't die long ago from heart attack or stroke!"

"So tell me how smart *that* was, little sister," Jimmy persisted. "As I said, you just didn't have the brain power. And if there's any doubt, just look at the trouble you had getting your drivers' license."

"Brain power had nothing to do with that," Tracey sputtered. "I was a victim of circumstances."

"As I recall," Nadine jumped in to aid in her daughter's vindication, "we forgot to take your birth certificate with us, so you went ahead and took the written test and then we returned home. The next day, for some reason that I don't remember, we went to a different motor vehicle division so you could take your road test. This time we took your birth certificate, but after standing in line for about an hour, we were informed that, because you had begun your testing elsewhere, all of your records were at the original location. You would have to return there to take the road test, or wait a few days until your paper work could be transferred."

"See?" gloated Tracey to her older brother. "I told you so! Don't forget, I was smart enough to be offered a scholarship to Utah State."

"Which you never used," Jimmy chided her gently. "Let's see, what was it for? Jump rope?"

"Dance! As you very well know!"

Abigail smirked. "I remember when your friends were talking about going to the awards night at the high school, where the scholarships would be announced. You told them you had to go to that, too, and they said, 'What are you going to do? Usher?'"

Jimmy snorted with glee, and Tracey glared at them both, then confronted Abigail. "Whose side are you on, anyway?"

Abigail pulled her mouth into a straight line and lifted her eyebrows. "Sorry, Sis, I got carried away in the moment." She then took a fork-full of potato salad, ruminating as she chewed. "I remember when Meese enrolled at Utah State." An instant temperance fell over the group at the mention of their esteemed sister. "I think her boyfriend followed her up there or something. Anyway, after Mom and Dad paid her tuition, as well as room and board for the semester, she decided she didn't want to go to college. So she got her tuition money refunded

159

(without so much as a word to Mom and Dad) and just stayed up there in the dorm, living the high life."

"I had no clue," complained Nadine. "I found out about it one day when I called to leave her a message, and she answered the telephone when she should have been in class." Nadine then turned to Lisa and chuckled. "I guess she wasn't *totally* perfect."

The nurse smiled. "I suspected as much."

"One thing about it," observed Tracey, "with the money she got back she bought us all some really nice Christmas presents that year!" They all chuckled softly, each of their minds returning briefly to those cherished days of Meese's happy association.

"Remember how much Meese loved mashed potatoes and gravy?" Abigail's voice was subdued. "I don't know how she stayed so tiny." Abigail paused for a moment as another thought brought tears to her eyes. "I remember her laugh; I wish I could hear it again."

Tracey nodded somberly. "She used to help me study my spelling words after we were in bed at night. I'd make up weird ways to pronounce them or give them funny meanings and it always made her laugh. Then we'd both get the giggles." Tracey smiled to herself, almost forgetting that there were others in the room. "I remember when she met Thayne. She was so in love." She turned to Nadine. "You never liked him much, did you?"

Nadine sighed. "It wasn't that I didn't like him. I think everyone liked Thayne. I just worried that they were too young to be so exclusively involved. I wanted Meese to date other boys and make sure she knew what she wanted before she got so serious."

"Well," Tracey continued, "he was my hero: the first man who ever looked out for me and made me feel protected." She gave Jimmy a sidelong glance. "It's for sure my big brother never did!" Jimmy was, for once, without a retort, so merely spluttered while the others grinned over his discomfiture.

"Remember, Jimmy, when you were about five, and the only thing you wanted for Christmas was a boat?" Nadine asked with a smile. "Dad and I talked to Grandpa Collins because he loved working with wood, and he agreed to build you one. He put together a cute little red tub, just your size, and Dad and I were so excited, thinking that we'd, for once, be able to give you just what you'd asked for. There'd be no disappointment that year! Ha! So we thought! But what you had in mind was something more along the lines of a forty-foot cabin cruiser."

Jimmy shrugged. "I always did think big."

"What I remember," complained Tracey, "is all those endless hours on Christmas morning, sitting on the basement stairs, waiting for Dad to get his camera lights set up so he could film us as we discovered what Santa had brought." The others nodded in abject agreement. "There I was, so excited I was peeing my pants, and Mom was standing at the top of the stairs, making us wait, and wait, and wait!"

"I guess my most memorable Christmas was in Idaho, when I got that broken down old motorcycle," Jimmy recalled. "I'd had a feeling I might get that rust bucket, but it was the only thing I really wanted. I remember waking up about five a. m. and creeping up the stairs from the basement, and out into the garage. I fiddled with it for some time, despite the cold and my bare feet. I couldn't wait for everyone to get up, so I could legally 'discover' what I got for Christmas and go spend more time on it.

"A few days later Dean and I (you remember him, the kid next door?), we got a real talking to about the lady in the neighborhood with the shotgun, who thought we were Hell's Angels coming to pillage and plunder, because we were riding our motorcycles around all the houses at 1:00 a. m. on New Years Day." Jimmy grinned at the others' laughter, then turned to Lisa. "This must be pretty boring for you, listening to us reminisce about old times."

But Lisa lifted a hand in contradiction. "Not at all. It makes me think of my own family gatherings. And, really, it's quite entertaining."

"So," asked Abigail, "are you planning to be with your family this Christmas?"

"Yes," Lisa smiled broadly, "I am. And I've imagined it to be just about like this."

"Do they live around here?" Tracey inquired.

"Yes. They're close by."

"I thought you said you were from out of state," protested Abigail.

"Oh, I am. But my family live here in the area."

"Too bad you're stuck here with us tonight," Jimmy commiserated. "I'm sure you'd rather be celebrating with your own brothers and sisters."

"It's really okay," Lisa assured him. "I don't mind at all."

"At least you won't have to travel far," noted Jimmy. "The roads are pretty treacherous right now."

Abigail chuckled over another emerging memory. "Jimmy, do you remember one day when you were left to tend us girls while Mom ran to the store? You must have been about ten. Anyway, it was the middle of winter and the roads were bad, so it took Mom longer than usual. And when she didn't return as soon as expected, you dialed four-one-one and asked the information operator, "Where's my mom?""

"Well," Jimmy came to his own defense, "it was her job to give out information, wasn't it? Made sense to me!"

"Mom, do you remember when I was about six or seven years old," Tracey inquired, "how we had to go outside to get downstairs to our bedrooms? You and Dad were building that addition on the back of the house to enclose the basement steps, and there wasn't any railing up yet. I must have been heading down to my bedroom and took a nosedive off the back porch. You remember that?"

"Of course I do! I'd never been so scared. You landed head first onto concrete, about ten feet below. I put you in bed with me that night, just to make sure you were all right. You kept waking up and crying out for 'Mama,' even though I was holding you the whole time and assuring you that I was right there." Nadine shook her head in wonder. "But the next morning you were fine, and never seemed to suffer any adverse aftereffects."

Jimmy hooted. "Hah! That's a matter of opinion!"

Tracey's mouth flew open in mock outrage as she turned to face him, playfully slugging him in the arm. "Brat!"

Jimmy held up his hands, affecting innocence. "How can you call me that, after all I used to do for you?"

"Like what? Tying me up to the piano? Or throwing my Wonder Woman underoos onto the roof? Or, let's see. Maybe you're thinking of the time you dumped hot chili on my foot."

"That was an accident!"

"Says you! And then, there was the family camping trip to Blue Lake."

Abigail laughed explosively. "I remember Blue Lake! That little mud hole in the Uintahs with about ten thousand bleating sheep adorning its banks. It rained every afternoon, complete with thunder and lightening and leaky tent, all of which terrified me."

"What terrified *me* was the 'bear' that crept around our tent at night!" groused Tracey.

Jimmy chuckled. "You have to admit it was a pretty good imitation. Ah, the family camp-outs. Did we ever have one when we weren't deluged with heavenly moisture?"

"You always had your own tent," Abigail pointed out, "and, if I remember right, yours was the only one that didn't leak. How did you manage that?"

Jimmy shrugged. "I was the only one with sufficient smarts to seal the seams."

Tracey grunted. "So why weren't you considerate enough to share your secrets?"

Jimmy laughed. "And deprive myself of the joy of your discomfort?"

"You might at least have had some concern for Mom and Dad."

"What can I say?" He put his next words to music, "I was a tender and callow fellow."

"Oh, pu-lease!" There was a short lull as everyone, once again, focused their attention on the slowly diminishing heaps of food, while allowing their minds a bit of time to retrieve the next flood of incriminating anecdotes. From time to time, throughout the evening, one of them would turn to their father. "You doin' okay, Pops?"

Melvin had never been one to participate verbally in any of their boisterous 'do you remember' sessions. In fact, when the grandchildren were very young, it was often his wont, during rowdy family gatherings, to disappear into his office with a good book. Now he merely nodded his contentment. Perhaps his loss of hearing had made their typical clamor more bearable.

"Remember the Idaho spud harvests?" asked Jimmy.

There was consensual groaning. "I remember the autumn when I was fifteen," remarked Abigail. "I worked in the harvest for the first time that year, riding the combine and sorting spuds. I think I earned about 300 dollars. Things were pretty tough that year and I remember Mom and Dad told us there wouldn't be any Christmas presents. Do you remember that, Mom?"

"I know that most of our years were pretty lean," Nadine acknowledged.

"Well, I decided that I'd give you the money I'd earned so that you could buy presents."

Nadine nodded. "I didn't want to take it. You'd worked hard for that money. I was sure you'd later regret it, when something came along that you needed for yourself."

"But I was never sorry. It made me feel happy to help out."

"Yes, I'm sure you benefitted more from your generosity than we did, although it sure felt good to know that there would be something under the tree after all."

"My favorite Christmas was the year Danny was born." Tracey looked adoringly at her brother. "I was so excited about having a baby brother, but, at the same time, I was so afraid that you weren't going to make it. I was also scared that Mom wouldn't come home from the hospital until, probably, the day after Christmas. When she showed up that morning, even though she had to leave you behind, it was the best present I ever had. Just seeing her, somehow validated your life; I felt then that everything would turn out okay. " Tracey turned her eyes toward her mother. "You'll never know, Mom, how happy it made me to have you home for Christmas."

Nadine's eyes filled. "I had no idea how important it was to you. I should have guessed; there are times when families just need to be together." Lisa handed her a Kleenex and she swiped it across her cheeks. "You remember when you all came to Thanksgiving dinner, our

165

first year in the dome home, and the carpet layers were working around our feet?"

"Wasn't that the year that Dale and Tracey's car disappeared?"

"That's right!" Nadine realized. "I'd almost forgotten. Dale had parked on our steep driveway, and after we'd finished eating and cleaning up, Tracey had gone down to get some photos she wanted to show us, that were in the glove compartment. I suddenly heard a frantic call, 'Mom! Where's my car?'

"We all hurried down the stairs and found Tracey gazing at the empty spot where the car had stood, a very puzzled look on her face. My first deduction was that it must have rolled down the road which ran perpendicular to our street, and led directly into our driveway. The decline from our house down that hill was intense. But my own car was parked at the bottom of the driveway, and it didn't seem possible that Tracey's could have escaped without crashing into mine. Nevertheless, I drove down to the bottom of the hill and surveyed the houses and yards on both sides of the street, but could see nothing unusual. My only conclusion was that the car must have been stolen. My thoughts were, 'The gall! For someone to come right up to the house, hot wire the car, and drive it away! How would anyone have the nerve?'

"I was just going in to call the police, when the phone rang. It was our neighbor, Steve. He wanted to know if we were missing an automobile. I asked him, 'Have you found Tracey's car?' 'Well, I have one here,' he said, 'upside down in my trees!'

"I walked down the hill to his home, while your dad called the police to report the incident. The car had, indeed, coasted down the driveway, leaving a microscopic spot of paint on the side of my Camaro, backed across the opposite neighbor's lawn and driveway, which sat slightly catty-cornered from us (we were, on closer inspection, able to discern some very clear tire marks), hit the small abutment at the top of a fifteen foot retaining wall and flipped over the edge, landing upside down between the two houses in a grove of scrub oak.

"The police soon arrived, and curious neighbors gathered. It turned into quite the social hour! When it finally broke up, Steve said to me, 'The next time you want to have a party, leave the car home!'"

Nadine then turned to her youngest daughter. "Tracey, tell the story about when you and Dale moved to Florida."

"Oh, my gosh, talk about trauma!"

Danny's curiosity was aroused. "How come I don't know anything about that?"

"I think you were at scout camp when it happened," Nadine explained, "and I guess you haven't been around any time when we've talked about it."

"So, what happened?"

Tracey shifted in her seat. "Well, as you know, Dale was in the air force and stationed at Mountain Home when we first got married. Then, not long after we lost our first baby, he got transferred to MacDill. So we rented a U-Haul to make the move. Dale drove the truck, and we pulled our car behind it. I got a portable kennel for Max, our German shepherd, and put him in the back seat of the car because, with Alan and Jaimee in the cab with us, there wasn't room for him in the truck. We stopped by Mom and Dad's on the way, and then, when we took off, I left my purse at their place."

Nadine took up the narrative. "I noticed the purse not long after they left, so your dad and I jumped into the car and headed east on I-80, trying to overtake them. We got all the way to Evanston without seeing any trace of their little convoy."

"We weren't really driving that fast," Tracey declared. "I figure we must have stopped for gas, or something, and Mom and Dad passed us."

"Anyway," Nadine continued, "we finally gave up and came home with the purse. A couple of days later I received this frantic collect phone call from somewhere in Missouri. Tracey was so hysterical she could hardly tell me what had happened. It turns out that, as they were traveling along a six lane highway at about seventy miles an hour, Dale happened to look into the rear view mirror just as Max jumped through the side window of their car. He had chewed his way through the metal cage, shredded the upholstery, and finally shattered the back window in his attempt to escape."

"Dale slammed on the brakes," Tracey exclaimed, "and we ran back and picked up the dog. He was bleeding everywhere. I put him across our laps, in the cab of the truck, and of course, he bled all over my brand new white pants that Dale had just bought me. The kids' clothes got some stains as well, but that didn't bother me too much."

"I'm not sure if she was more upset about Max, or about the pants," chimed in Dale.

Tracey chuckled. "I was so mad at that stupid dog by then, my pants seemed the more valuable of the two. So, we pulled into the first truck stop we saw and I tried to locate a vet who would make a house call. Since I'd left my purse behind, we had no cash and no credit cards, except the one belonging to the air force that could only be used for gas and food."

"Hence, the call to me for help," Nadine explained.

"Mom gave me her credit card number, and I finally found a vet who was willing to come and treat Max at the truck stop. The dog was ripped up pretty badly, but no broken bones, which was amazing. The vet stitched and bandaged him, and gave me some tranquilizers (for the dog, although I could have used some, myself). The pills were supposed to keep him relaxed and quiet until we got to Florida."

Nadine chortled. "Tracey was so shaken by the whole thing that she overdosed the dog, and by the time they got to Florida, he was so loopy he couldn't stand up."

All but Danny had heard the episode told and retold, but it was still worth a good laugh (one of those traumatic incidents that eventually earns its way to the rank of humor).

"So, was the dog okay after that?" asked Danny.

"He was fine," Tracey assured him. "Lived to a ripe old age."

Danny shook his head. "I sure missed out on a lot, being the caboose." He sent a rueful look in Nadine's direction.

"Well, now," she protested, "who do you think is to blame for the long interval between Tracey and you? I certainly wasn't the one dragging my feet. I think you were up there in heaven, just bidin' your time, supposing that if you waited long enough, you might get a better offer!"

"Nah," objected Danny. "I was just waiting for the family to get pure enough to associate with perfection!"

This was met with the expected whoops of derision.

"Remember when Danny was a yell leader at Snow College?" Tracey asked of everyone in general.

"I remember he always choked when I called it 'cheerleading,'" remarked Nadine. "And I remember he broke his sternum, lifting those girls."

Danny smirked. "They were cows."

"Oh, I saw a couple of them who came to visit you that summer. They didn't look to me like cows."

Danny gave his mother a sidelong glance. "Trust me, Mom; they were cows."

Somehow, during all of the babble, the family had been able to finish their meals, and began stacking plates and re-covering bowls. "We need to have a picture taken!" declared Abigail. "Who knows when we'll get another chance? Tracey, you've got your camera, don't you?" The answer to that was predictable; Tracey *always* had her camera.

Abigail turned toward the nurse. "Lisa, would you mind doing the honors?"

"No, no!" objected Nadine. "I want her to be in it with us."

They were all a little startled by their mother's vociferous request, but Tracey shrugged and said, "Okay, I'll go see if I can find someone." She pulled open the heavy door and peered in each direction, then purposefully headed to the right, returning shortly with a recruited amateur photographer in tow.

The family squeezed in around Nadine's bed and effected the mandatory smiles, while the nurse clicked away; she insisted on taking more than one, just to make sure. Tracey retrieved her camera, offered the woman her thanks, and then helped Abigail place the remains of their meal into plastic bags to be transported home. "Danny," she said, "you can come home with us, and stay there until you have to go back. I have plenty of room."

Danny slung his arm across his sister's shoulders. "Thanks, Trace, but I think I'll stay here with Mom for a while."

Tracey pulled a pencil and paper from her purse and began writing. "Well, take our phone numbers, then, and call when you need someone to come and get you. Dinner tomorrow is at two o'clock."

Danny took the proffered paper. "Don't worry," he smiled, "I'll be in touch."

"Before you all go, I want you to promise me something," Nadine entreated. They stopped what they were doing and turned to face her. "I want you to promise that you'll spend tomorrow together as a family, no matter what."

"We're already planning on that, Mom," Abigail assured her.

"Humor an old lady, and just give me your word."

Tracey smiled and patted her arm. "Of course, Mom, we promise. Cross our hearts and hope to die."

"I'm serious, Tracey."

Tracey eyed her mother quizzically, then sat on the bed beside her. "So am I, Mom. I give you my word, we'll be together for dinner tomorrow."

They each, in turn, bade their mother farewell and wearily headed for home.

"Oh, Meese." Nadine took the young woman's hands in her own. "Thank you for the best night of my life. What a wonderful gift you gave us." She shifted her head on the pillows. "Do you think anyone suspected the truth?"

"If they did, they immediately discounted it; people have a difficult time believing anything other than their own reality."

"Hmm. I wish I could have told them."

Lisa smiled. "I'm sure that, before long, they'll know."

Nadine reached out her other hand to Danny, who stood on the opposite side of the bed. "I'm so glad you're here."

"Are you ready to go home now, Mom?" he asked.

Nadine sighed happily. "I guess it's time; I've just had my going away party. What a blessing that all of my family were here to wish me bon voyage, although I'm sure they didn't realize that's what they were doing." She offered a feeble smile to these two precious ones, and with

171

their hands clasped in her own, slowly closed her eyes as the last breath of mortality gradually seeped from her lungs.

Abigail, at home now, had put away the left-over food, and though it was the wee hours, was sleepily loading the last of the plates into the dishwasher when the phone rang. "I'm sorry to have to tell you," said the voice on the other end, "but your mother passed on about fifteen minutes ago."

"She died?" Abigail gasped, as she flumped into the nearest chair. "Are you sure? We were just with her, and she seemed so well."

"That's not entirely unheard of. Occasionally one of our residents will experience a brief respite just before they cross over. I thought you might like to come and sit with her for a few minutes before the people from the funeral home arrive."

"Yes, thank you. We'll be right there."

Abigail sat for a moment, hardly able to process the idea of her mother's demise. She had, over the last year or so, secretly, and not altogether selfishly, wished for this moment to arrive, but after the happy time they had just spent together, it seemed incomprehensible, not to mention unjust, that this should be the time for it to happen. And on Christmas, as well! A sudden thought flitted across her mind. Had her mother known? Is that why she was so adamant about extracting her children's promise that they would spend the day together? Surely not; she had felt so well, there couldn't have been any premonition of doom. It must have just been her usual desire that her family be there for one another, and spend time together.

Abigail reached for the telephone, dialed Tracey's number, apprised her sister of the regrettable news, and made arrangements to meet at the care center. On the way to retrieving her coat from the closet, she stopped in the doorway of the living room, where her family was winding down from the late-night events. Seeing her there, leaning somberly against the door frame, Barry paused mid-sentence and eyed her quizzically. "What's up?" he asked.

"That was the care center. Mom just died."

Barry stood and moved toward his wife, put his arms around her and pulled her head to his shoulder. "I'm sorry."

Jimmy was incredulous. "That's impossible! She was fine thirty minutes ago!"

Abigail lifted her head and nodded. "It's almost like she was just waiting to have the family all together so she could say goodbye." She humphed softly. "Mom almost got the family picture she always wanted; if only Meese had been there." She straightened up and wiped at her eyes. "I almost forgot, I need to call Dad to see if he wants to go with us to the center. Tracey is going to meet me there. You feel like coming, Jimmy?"

"Of course," Jimmy accepted.

Melvin, when Abigail phoned, begged off, claiming an upset stomach. "I'll say my goodbyes tomorrow," he declared, "when I'm feeling better."

The three siblings arrived at the center simultaneously and walked together toward their mother's room. "Dad couldn't come?" Tracey asked.

"He said he wasn't feeling well, but I wonder if maybe he was just a little afraid. I worry about him, too, about what this will do to him."

When the three of them entered Nadine's room, she looked as if she were merely asleep, and they automatically tiptoed to each side of her bed. "I wonder where Danny is," noted Tracey.

"He probably got a hotel room for the night, and left before this happened," Jimmy reasoned.

"I told him he could stay with us," Tracey pointed out.

"I know, but he maybe didn't want to put you out."

"That's silly. He knows he's always welcome."

Jimmy merely shrugged. After a few moments of silent thought, Abigail glanced down at the side table upon which Nadine's meager belongings rested: eyeglasses, a plastic cup of water, a CD player that Abigail had brought in during the early days of her mother's confinement. She had hoped that Nadine might enjoy listening to the books she could no longer read for herself. It had been an exercise in futility, like so many other of her efforts.

Abigail reached over and lifted Nadine's bracelet from the table, noticing in the process a slip of paper that lay underneath containing a short written message: "Abby, your mother wanted you to have this." She laid the heavily adorned silver cable across her palm and absently slid the charms, one by one, from right to left. "I don't think she ever took this off," she mused. Then, as she fingered one of the amulets, she tilted her head quizzically. "There's a new charm here." She looked up at Tracey. "Did you get Mom a charm this year?"

"Of course. Didn't you?"

"When did you give it to her?"

Tracey scowled at her sister. "I didn't. Not yet. I was going to do it today."

Abigail turned to her brother. "Jimmy?"

He shrugged. "Not me. That's strictly your province."

Abigail lifted the bracelet, indicating the cause of her bafflement. "I've never seen this one before."

Her brother and sister leaned in for a closer look. "A soldier," Tracey intoned. She straightened and looked at Abigail, each of them startled by the same thought. "Danny?"

Abigail shrugged. "Who else could it be?"

"But when did he have time to get it?"

"Maybe Lisa told him about the bracelet and he brought the charm with him last night." Suddenly Abigail started. "Did Danny leave us a phone number? We need to let him know."

Tracey grimaced. "I gave him our numbers, but I didn't get one from him. Since he's been gone so long, I didn't even think about him having a cell phone."

Abigail's shoulders slumped as she racked her brain for a way to locate her kid brother. Then she lifted her head. "Lisa must know how to get hold of him; she's the one who found him in the first place. We'll ask at the front desk and see if she's still here somewhere." Abigail looked again at the treasured bracelet and began to drop it into her purse, when her eyes fell upon yet another unfamiliar charm. "There's one more that wasn't here before: an angel. Do you suppose Lisa–?"

Tracey again shrugged. "Who knows. She did seem pretty fond of Mom."

"But why an angel?"

"Angel of mercy, maybe?"

Abigail twisted her mouth to one side. "You know, as much as we all liked her, that's still a little presumptuous to put herself there amidst the symbols of Mom's children."

"Does it truly matter at this point?"

Abigail gave it some thought. "I guess not; not really."

"She was sure a lot like our Meese," Tracey reflected.

Abigail nodded. "I have to admit, it was almost like having our sister back." She paused for a long moment. "You don't think it's possible that–"

"What?"

Abigail sighed wistfully. "Oh, nothing. I guess we should be going while there's still a chance to catch Lisa before she leaves."

When they inquired at the receptionist's desk, however, they were met with a blank stare. "Lisa? I don't believe we have a Lisa working here."

"She's new," Abigail informed her. "I think she's only been here for the last ten days or so. She works the night shift."

"Let me check the computer." The woman tapped a few keys, frowned, and shook her head. "Could you have the name wrong?"

"No!" Tracey's response was sharp. "She was here last night. She came on at eleven. Maybe she's not a nurse. Maybe she's a CNA or something."

"According to the schedule, Suzanne was on duty last night. Her shift hasn't ended yet. Let me see if I can locate her for you."

Abigail sat and Tracey paced, while the receptionist activated the loud speaker system and paged Suzanne. A few minutes later a young woman appeared through the double doors; the sisters recognized her immediately as their personal photographer of the night before. "Thank goodness," breathed Abigail as she stood and approached the nurse. "We were here last night visiting Nadine."

Suzanne nodded. "Yes, I remember. You asked me to take your picture."

"That's right. We need to locate the other nurse who was on duty, the one who was in Mom's room with us. Her name is Lisa."

Suzanne's frown was disconcerting. "I don't know any Lisa," she replied.

"She posed with us for the picture," Tracey reminded her in a tone which was becoming agitated.

Suzanne shook her head. "I think you're mistaken."

Abigail was becoming irrepressibly exasperated. "Mom even made a point of making sure Lisa was in it with the rest of us."

Suzanne's expression was that of skepticism. "I'm sorry, but to the best of my knowledge, your mom didn't say anything at all."

Tracey threw up her arms and turned to walk away, then halted suddenly. "Wait," she snapped, making an about face. "My camera's still in my bag. I can show you her picture." Tracey plowed through the contents of her purse, finally rescuing her Konica from its depths. "Here," she crowed, walking toward Suzanne as she flipped on the power and scrolled through the contents of the memory card. Then she stopped short. "Wait a minute. It's got to be in here." She clicked back and forth through the images, bewilderment showing clearly on her face. "I don't understand. The pictures aren't here." She looked helplessly at Abigail and handed her the camera.

"But that's impossible," uttered Abigail as she repeated her sisters actions. "Did you already download them onto your computer?"

"No. I was going to do that today. Either they got erased somehow, or my camera malfunctioned. So, what do we do now?"

Suzanne was apologetic. "I'm sorry I couldn't help you."

Abigail nodded, "Yeah, well."

The three siblings left the facility in frustration. "I swear, Alzheimer's must be contagious," Abigail grumbled. "I think everyone in this place has lost their senses."

"Well, since Danny didn't choose to stay at my house tonight—or I guess it's 'last night' now—I think you're right, Jimmy; he must be at a hotel close by," noted Tracey. "Let's split up the phone book and do some telephoning. If that doesn't work, we'll go to plan B."

"Which is?"

Tracey sighed. "I wish I knew."

An hour later the short list of area hotels was exhausted, with still no trace of their baby brother. Abigail phoned Tracey in defeat. "Well," she reasoned, "the only thing we can do is wait for him to contact us. By the way, would you hate it if we cancelled dinner today? I'm not really in the mood."

"Abby," admonished Tracey, "we promised Mom."

"But none of us knew what was going to happen then."

"If you remember, she made a point of 'no matter what.'"

"Yeah, I've been thinking about that."

"Anyhow," Tracey continued. "Jimmy's come all this way and I've already put the turkey into the oven. It's what Mom would want."

"I suppose you're right. Well, then, I'll see you at two."

Abigail moved to the living room, where Jimmy and Marlene were relaxing on the couch, while Barry sat in the overstuffed chair. Presents still lay, all but forgotten, beneath the tree. Barry looked up as she entered. "No luck?" he queried.

Abigail stopped at the end of the sofa and stood with arms folded. "We called every hotel in the area; I don't know what else to do. Hopefully, Danny'll telephone today. I'm thinking he'll probably go back to the rest home before long, and we'll undoubtedly hear from him then. Meanwhile, we're going ahead with dinner." She gazed at the gaily wrapped gifts, yesterday a symbol of joy and love, today a mockery of her sorrow. "Maybe we can put off opening presents until tonight. Right now we'd better try to get some sleep."

With nodded agreement her brother and his wife headed toward their quarters, while she and Barry did the same. He draped his arm across her shoulders and gave a little squeeze. "Are you sure you're all right?"

Abigail compatibly leaned into the comfort of his body. "I will be. The whole thing seems so surreal." Having reached their bedroom, they sat close to each other on the edge of the bed, Barry's arm still offering solace. Abigail sighed. "It doesn't seem possible that it was only a few hours ago that we were all laughing and joking together. And having Danny there: that was incredible. Do you realize how many years it's been?"

"I have a pretty good idea."

Abigail patted her husband's knee. "We'd better call it a night. I'll never make it through dinner if we don't get some sleep."

But sleep would not come for Abigail. Her mind continued to replay the scenes from her childhood, both those that had been dredged up by her family's chatter, and others which had almost been forgotten. Mostly she thought of Meese and the long-ago, late-night confabs through which she and her sisters had cried, and giggled, as they poured out their hearts to each other. There had never been any secrets between them, not while Meese was alive.

A tear trickled onto Abigail's pillow as she recalled one school morning when they were teen-agers. She hadn't been able to arouse Meese, and had run downstairs to summon her mom. Nadine was fixing breakfast and Tracey was already at the table. Abby had cried frantically, "Mom, I can't wake up Meese!" Nadine had dropped everything and the three of them had rushed up the stairs and burst into the girls' bedroom, their faces clearly showing the panic that gripped them.

Nadine had run to the bedside and grasped her inert daughter's shoulders, shaking her gently and calling her name. Suddenly, a grin broke across Meese's face and her body began to shake with laughter. That was the only time Abigail remembered ever truly being angry with

179

her sister; she hadn't thought her little prank to be one bit funny. It wasn't many years later that Abigail experienced that same soul-wrenching terror over Meese, but that time it was no joke.

Her thoughts then turned to the day of that fateful phone call, when she'd been told that Danny was missing. It was all too much. How was it possible that they had managed to go on with their lives? Well, her mom hadn't, not really. She'd found a way to escape into Never-never Land, where her children had never grown up: never gone away to war, never suffered from their own bad choices, never died in a car wreck.

Abigail wiped a hand across her wet cheek, and glanced at the clock. It was still earlier than she needed to get up, but she knew that remaining in bed for another hour, or so, would do her no good; she would only continue to thrash about. With drooping eyelids and emotions she made her way to the bathroom, drowsed through her typical three minute shower, brushed her teeth and hair, and pulled on a pair of slacks and a sweater. Then, minimally revitalized, she slowly trudged to the kitchen.

Her assignment for today was a Jello salad, pumpkin pies and orange rolls (thank goodness for Rhodes thirty minute variety). Fortunately, the salad was already in the fridge, so needed no further attention, but she'd left the other preparations until today, wanting everything to be freshly made. As exhausted as she was, and as difficult as it would be to get into the spirit of holiday baking, she'd better get started on the task. She actually wanted nothing more than to go back to bed and dissolve into unconsciousness (were that possible). She certainly didn't feel up to a celebration, but it would be criminal, she supposed, to disregard what now seemed to be her mother's deathbed request.

While the rolls were baking, she lined the pie pans with pastry and mixed the filling. Then, as the pies took their turn in the oven, she iced the rolls and checked her e-mails. Thirteen new messages: four from coworkers, who, it seemed, couldn't even take Christmas off, and the rest of them junk.

One by one, Barry and their two house guests gradually pulled themselves from their beds, stumbled their way through the morning's hygienic rituals, and then followed their noses into the kitchen. "Sorry there's not enough milk for cereal," Abigail apologized, as she rose from the computer. "What else can I get you?"

"Just show us the way to toast and orange juice," Jimmy said with a wave of his hand. "That'll hold us 'til dinner."

Eventually, all was ready for the trek to Tracey's house. Abigail's son Paul and family arrived shortly and stood in the entry with coats on while the others grabbed their wraps. Abigail expected that the temperatures would drop dramatically before they left Tracey's to return home that night, so she went to her room to retrieve her wool scarf.

There on the bed was an unwelcome, brightly-wrapped gift. She huffed and rolled her eyes. Hadn't she told Barry that she didn't want to bother with presents until tonight? She glanced at the tag and was surprised to find it addressed to Jimmy, Abby and Tracey, with boldly written instructions that they were to open it together. She took her scarf from the closet and carried it, along with the strange package into the living room. "Do you know anything about this, Barry?" she asked accusingly.

"What is it?"

Abigail smirked. "If I knew that, I wouldn't be asking you about it." Barry forgave her insolence, and calmly denied any knowledge of the parcel in question.

"How about you, Jimmy?" But Jimmy shook his head.

181

"Okay," she conceded. "Then let's load up and be on our way."

The men helped her stow the food into the back of Barry's SUV, and the four of them climbed in. Then, with Paul and Jocelyn's family following in their car, they headed for Tracey's house, with a stop along the way to pick up Melvin.

While Tracey held open her front door, Barry and Jimmy transmitted the dishes from car to house. Then Abigail crossed the threshold, carrying the mysterious present. "What's in the package?" asked Tracey suspiciously. She and Abigail had decided long ago that exchanging gifts between families was an unnecessary extravagance. The real gift, the important gift, was the time they spent together.

"That's what we're going to find out," Abigail replied as the two of them made their way to the kitchen.

"Just toss your coats in the guest room," Tracey called to the others, then turned her attention back to her sister.

"I found this on my bed, just before we left," Abby explained. "It's addressed to you and Jimmy and me, and everyone in my household disclaims any knowledge of it, whatsoever. Of course, I'm too tired to care if they're lying. Have you heard from Danny yet?"

"No! And I'm a little bit ticked. Didn't I tell him we'd eat at two?" She leaned over and pulled down the oven door, releasing the delicious aroma of Christmas goodness, as she lifted out the turkey and set it on the counter.

"I'm sure you did," Abigail affirmed. "Something must have come up. Maybe he had to report back unexpectedly."

"Well, let's hope not; one night just wasn't long enough. He should have, at least, been able to stay through today."

"Either way, I'm sure we'll hear from him soon."

Tracey nodded. "At least we know he's okay." She opened the refrigerator and handed salads out to Abigail, which she, in turn, carried to the table. "Okay," Tracey declared, "I can't stand it any more; let's get at this mystery package."

When everyone had settled in the living room, Abigail thrust the cryptic gift toward her brother. "Jimmy, you're the oldest; how about you doing the honors?"

Jimmy took the package, and Abigail seated herself in a chair close by. As he pulled off the paper she could see that it was a framed picture of some sort, but couldn't determine the subject. Jimmy grinned and gave Tracey a knowing smirk. "Well, aren't you the sneaky one!" he accused her.

"What!" she asked in all innocence.

Slowly he turned the picture around for them all to see. Abigail's eyes widened. She swivelled to face Tracey, who was doing an excellent job of feigning ignorance. "You told me your camera malfunctioned! And all the time you were planning to surprise us. I have to admit, you did a pretty convincing job of acting. So, which one of my sneaky family did you recruit to smuggle it into my house?"

Abigail stood and crossed to Jimmy, then took the picture to have a closer look, while Tracey closed in behind her. "This is really a good shot," admired Abigail. "Almost professional. But why the changes? And when did you find time to PhotoShop?"

Tracey's expression was still one of bewilderment. "I have no idea what you're talking about," she stated adamantly.

"Okay, Tracey, you can quit your pretending now. We're too old for Santa Claus."

"I'm not kidding; I didn't do this!"

Abigail looked askance at her sister. "It had to be your camera that took the picture. Who else could have done it?"

Tracey grabbed the photo from her sister and stared, uncomprehending, at the image, her brow furrowed. Each member of the family was positioned just as she remembered; Dad was in the chair next to the bed, where Mom relaxed against the pillows. The rest of them were closely huddled in, their animated faces exhibiting the gaiety of the night's activity, and each of them looking as if someone had just cracked a joke (and, probably, someone had).

But here was the baffling part: Lisa was not in her patterned scrubs, nor Danny in battle fatigues. Instead, Lisa wore a simple dress, and Danny a tailored suit, both of which were white: immaculate, dazzling, luminous white. Their faces glowed with an ethereal radiance, and their expressions were beatific.

Tracey lifted moist eyes to her sister. "Abby?" She moved her head slowly from side to side, unable to articulate the thoughts that were bombarding her mind.

Abigail, after thoughtfully regarding her younger sibling's tearful countenance, turned toward Jimmy, who slowly stood and wrapped an arm around each of them, his own eyes suspiciously bright. Tracey was the first to speak. "It isn't possible, is it?"

Abigail gazed once more at the photograph, her fuzzy vision blurring the individual outlines, so that the separate figures seemed to meld into a single, indivisible unit. Then, with a tender smile, she murmured, "Who could have imagined that it would be Meese and Danny who at last gave Mom her wish: all of us finally together for a family portrait."

Acknowledgments

Many, many thanks to:

My Daughter Tami for always being available to me as my own personal editor, and for the countess hours she has spent reading, critiquing, suggesting, encouraging, and supporting.

My Family for being my captive audience, and reading everything I write (whether they want to or not), for always offering their love and respect, and, finally, for their dependability, honesty, and integrity.

My Faithful Friends for standing by me in times of tragedy, for keeping my head above the quicksand, my feet above the ground, and my soul above the depths of despair.

My Heavenly Father for endowing me with the talents and abilities that have blessed my life.

About the Author

Nannette was born in Southern California and spent her first seventeen years playing on the beach (except when school interrupted). She then enrolled at BYU as a music major, with a minor in English. She married during her junior year and returned to California to settle into married life and begin raising a family (her number one priority).

Following the birth of her third child she and her husband moved their small household back to the Rocky Mountains, where they subsequently added seven more children to their family.

Finally, after thirty years of diapers and tricycles, she resumed her education, this time at the University of Utah, where she graduated summa cum laude with a BS in psychology. Her purpose in writing, other than the pure joy that it brings, is to offer the reader a page turning alternative to that which is vulgar and profane.

Printed in Great Britain
by Amazon